"A Cold Day for Murder"

A Cozy Mystery

Lost in Alaska Series
Volume One

Leigh Mayberry

© 2019
Leigh Mayberry

Edition v1.00 (2019.08.30)

Special thanks to the following volunteer readers who helped with proofreading: Christine S., Kari Wellborn, M. McMath, Dick B., RB, JayBee, Julie Pope, and those who assisted but wished to be anonymous. Thank you so much for your support.

Chapter One

When Cheryl and Brian Snyder made their daily trek to the Midnight Sun Café on Shore Avenue, Nancy was usually already in the kitchen prepping ovens, checking inventory and refrigeration temperatures. It was a routine they shared since Brian bought out the owner of the restaurant five years ago, using their combined retirement accounts on a vision of the future that somehow had to do with serving greasy burgers and fries to the villagers and thinking that life was going to be more relaxed in the north.

"When did you last talk to Nancy?" Cheryl asked. It wasn't a loaded question, Brian and Nancy usually stayed later than Cheryl, one of them had to be a parent to their precocious ten-year-old.

"We closed up around eight last night." Brian turned on the rest of the lights in the dining area. He checked the bathrooms and collected the napkin dispensers to refill.

Cheryl started the first round of coffee in the commercial coffee machines. They had two antiquated brewers. Most of the morning, customers put more cream and sugar in their cups than coffee. They didn't make any money on beverages, but they had to compete with the hotel and the trader store. The competition was supposed to be good for business. In a town with three thousand year-round residents, anyone selling coffee other than the Midnight Sun Café put them deeper in red.

"Did you call her yet?" Cheryl shouted from the walk-in cooler.

"Why do I have to call her? She's your sister."

The cooler door slammed, much to Brian's displeasure. Cheryl didn't have a sense of what it meant to take it easy on equipment. Maintaining refrigeration in town was hard enough without the added stress on the doors because someone was ornery about employment problems within the company.

Brian pulled the smartphone from his pocket; hit the contact number on speed dial. Wedging the phone between his ear and shoulder, he continued to fill the napkin dispensers. "No answer."

"She's probably got a guy over there." Cheryl lived vicariously through her sister. Nancy had charisma, was slimmer than Cheryl and younger by ten years. She'd moved out of town for the first part of her life once high school was over. Like most kids who had no clear direction or focus to kick-start her life, she'd come back to town, on her sister and brother-in-law's dimes to work off her debt until she had another break or someone to latch onto for the next part of her life. Until then, Cheryl and Nancy talked about her lovers, knew about the few men in town who had secret crushes on her sister, and for some reason, it was enough for Cheryl to watch at a distance as someone lived an exciting life instead of trying to have one herself.

"Do you want to go wake her up?" Brain called from the dining room, replacing the dispensers. He didn't wait for Cheryl to answer before adding, "You know, we don't have to pay her if she doesn't come in."

"You know how Mondays are!" Temper up, frustrated with the business and balancing the relationship where nepotism got in the way of commerce, Cheryl used the inanimate objects in the

4

kitchen to take out her aggravation with hiring her sister to wait tables and schmooze with the customers.

Brian would never admit it, but Nancy was good for business. Even if she was always late, usually wanted loans against her weekly paychecks, and had a carte blanche attitude when it came to lovers, she drew in crowds to the restaurant. People liked her. It wasn't only men, single and married, who came to ogle his sister-in-law, women liked Nancy. Because she had a no-nonsense attitude about life, Nancy didn't have a lot of filters when it came to casting light on acquaintances.

"Where are you going?" Brian asked when the plastic plates dropped on the steel counter in the kitchen. Cheryl moved around to the dining area and headed for the door. She slipped on the heavy coat while she fumed.

"You know we need her here."

"I'll go with you," Brian said. He snagged his coat from the back of the booth near the door. He switched off the overhead restaurant lights before leaving and locking up. "I want to check the coffee prices at the hotel this morning."

"You're not going to compete with them," Cheryl said, her voice tinged with anger. "They're getting their supplies in from Anchorage."

"How do you know?"

"I talked to Cindy. She told me Bill and Mona are modeling the hotel after the one on Fifth Avenue. They got on the hotel supply list for discounts. They're ordering another espresso machine."

"Shit," Brian hissed. "Are they looking to franchise?" He climbed into the Chevy pick-up. Cheryl climbed into the passenger seat. It took two turns of the key to getting the engine to fire up.

"You should have plugged in the truck last night," Cheryl complained.

"Weather was supposed to start to break."

They continued to bicker as Brian pulled onto Shore Avenue and headed for the apartment complex where Nancy lived in a one-bedroom on the third floor.

It was a little after five in the morning. Nancy never liked mornings, complained when she had to open. She lived the life of a nocturnal creature, and while that worked for winter months, during the summer, Nancy taped cardboard to the windows in the apartment to block out the midnight sun. Many of the units left cardboard or aluminum foil over the windows year-round, why remove it when it had to go back up again in a few months?

Mountain Manor was a thirty-unit, three-story apartment building without an elevator. There was ramp access to the first floor, and anyone who needed a place with no stairs was on a six-year waiting list. Nancy was young, fit, and she considered the daily stair climbing exercise.

Brian and Cheryl went through the side door, closest to the stairwell. There was a keycode electronic lock, and everyone in town had the codes. People talked in a small town. Guests didn't need to ring when they visited. Texting worked; people shared the system. It was a false sense of security and just part of day to day life above the Arctic Circle.

6

"You got your key?" Brian asked. He'd tried the doorknob when Nancy didn't answer after the third round of knocking. There was a lingering scent of cigarettes and a mild layer of marijuana smoke in the hallway.

Cheryl dug through her purse until she produced a key ring with two keys. One for Nancy's Honda four-wheeler, which was still parked outside with a crust of frost coating it, and another key for the apartment that Cheryl slipped in the doorknob and turned.

Inside the small apartment, it looked as if Nancy had company. The small round dining table near the door was set with two plates, and two glasses.

"Nancy! Yo, Nancy! Let's go!" Brian felt every minute they wasted collecting Cheryl's sister was a dollar they could earn on coffee for customers. He wandered down the hallway while Cheryl, collected the plates and glasses and put them in the dishwasher, she couldn't help but clean-up after her sister.

Nancy already had the washer at full capacity, and by the time Cheryl put in the rest of the dishes and added detergent she was left with no choice but to switch it on and turned around.

"Oh my God," she stammered. Brian stood close to her; he had somehow returned to the kitchenette without her hearing him. "What's wrong?"

His face was alabaster, his brown eyes rimmed with red. "Call the police."

Chapter Two

Meghan Sheppard knew how to start with the word "king" add a "guy" with the French pronunciation, with a double dose of a "Kiya" for the ending. Kinguyakkii, Alaska wasn't hard to pronounce once someone said it for you a few times. It was a five-syllable word in Inuit which translated into Northern Lights. She'd memorized it when it wasn't necessary because Meghan believed in the importance of traditions, even when they weren't her own.

The smartphone rang a little after seven in the morning. Anywhere else the sun would already be up, cresting mountains or skyscrapers, not in this town, thirty-three miles above the Arctic Circle. In March sunrise wasn't expected until after nine, at least until Daylight Savings added an hour to the schedule.

"What's up?" Meghan dropped the standard address a few months after she got hired for the job. It turned out her staff wasn't big on protocol when it came to phone etiquette. Rather than waste more time trying to get her team to play by her rules. Meghan had a lot to learn about the game they were playing because it was older than most games she knew about in her years of law enforcement.

"Hey Chief," Lester said. He worked overnight and was supposed to have Oliver relieve him for the morning shift. "We got a thing over at the Manor."

"Okay," she said, drawing out the word. Lester talked to most people in a way that suggested they were already in the middle of a conversation before someone spoke to him.

"Yeah, you should get over there, Chief."

"Can you give me a clue before I head there?"

Lester and Oliver addressed Meghan as 'Chief' because it was technically accurate. She felt that it was somehow insulting to their Native Alaskan sensibility. There were some words just shouldn't be used anymore in the English language.

Her officers were tenth or eleventh generation Inuit. Native Alaskans who'd spend every breath of their lives in and around Kinguyakkii. Two men, who grew up together, knew everyone in the township and the surrounding villages. The kind of deputies she wanted because they could identify people at a distance by the color and style of their fur hats, or Ushankas as the Russians called the cold-weather caps. If they called her "Chief" it had nothing to do with Native American stereotyping, it had to do with the fact she was the Chief of Police for Kinguyakkii— the Town of Northern Lights. She forced herself to get used to it.

"Brian Snyder called Oliver. He said that he and Cheryl went to their sister Nancy's apartment." It was one of those mornings where Lester was going to make three left turns to go right. "Oliver said that Brian told him they found Nancy in bed."

"Okay," she said again, "and?"

"She's dead, Chief."

***

Meghan had a promising career as a Special Agent in the FBI. She admittedly loved the bifold black leather ID wallet, and flashing her credentials at important events, like terrorist strikes, crime scenes and crazy Black Friday sales at the department store in Syracuse, New York, where Meghan was before she left the real world and took the job in Kinguyakkii.

The trouble was, Meghan never saw terrorist activity, never hunted a serial killer, she once flashed her credentials at a Black Friday event, but it was only to get to the front of the line before the store opened.

After eight years as 'Special Agent,' Meghan lost interest in tracking predatory offenders who defrauded the government when they reused a postage stamp twice because the machine didn't postmark the letters directly. The title was impressive, and the work was mundane. At least until the night, she got shot.

"You checked the body?"

"Yeah, Chief, she's dead all right, a little blue too."

Immediately Meghan started considering what happened to the woman. Blue tones meant a lack of oxygen. "Make sure no one gets into the apartment, Lester." Meghan stayed on the phone the entire time she'd leaped from bed, struggled with yesterday's jeans, debated briefly to change her panties before putting on the layers of clothes it took to go out into the environment and manage to stay warm.

"I got a sign on the wall in the stairwell."

"What sign?"

"Housekeeping had a 'Wet Floor' sign lying around," he said, "Should keep people from coming upstairs."

"Call Oliver, have him bring over the forensic kit from the office." She didn't wait for Lester to answer.

By the time Meghan went through the front door, she saw the frost had built up on the windshield of the Chevy Suburban. She hadn't plugged in the engine block heater last night because people were talking in town, mentioned how the weather was supposed to change.

When she finally got the engine to fire up for the Chevy, Meghan wondered if they were talking about it getting colder instead of warmer. Either way, she had to wait for the windshield to defrost because the ice scraper she had in the truck broke when it was —5 F° for a week straight in January.

Sitting behind the wheel of the freezing truck, heater on full, blasting icy air in her face before the coils heated up, Meghan reflected on her time in Kinguyakkii.

Somehow Meghan ended up in a village on the top of the world where people referred to the rest of the United States as 'the lower-forty-eight.' She took the job because it sounded like an adventure. The divorce was final, she was forty-six years old, and while law enforcement still appealed to her, she wanted something that sang a different tune than mail fraud, or the occasional federal subpoena service. US Marshal sounded exciting until Meghan found out that apprehending wanted fugitives happened about as often as a hit movie came out with title cards that had better fonts than the actual business. Air Marshals spent entirely too much time off-earth. While Meghan liked to travel in moderation, she felt more secure when she did the driving, and her vehicle was on the ground.

She didn't complain. People here were friendly, for the most part. There were occasional bouts of domestic violence, some issues with alcohol, usually both at the same time. Kinguyakkii was a place Meghan never knew existed until it showed up in an internet search for a career change. Exotic locations didn't always include sunny beaches and tropical weather.

It was a balmy 26°F with the high expected around 45°F and a clear day with a little more sunlight than yesterday, by about seven minutes. In another month the town would get twenty-four hours of daylight for about forty days, better than forty days of rain, Meghan considered.

Once the ice melted from the windshield enough for her to see, Meghan turned on the police flashers on the Chevy, pulled out of the driveway and sped across town to where Lester held back the crowds with a 'Wet Floor' sign and the Town of Northern Lights saw its first possible murder in fifteen years.

Chapter Three

The crowd consisted of mostly renters from the third floor, Cheryl and Brian Snyder, and Officer Lester Graves. By the time Meghan arrived, Officer Oliver Henry pulled up on the Polaris four-wheeler he drove most of the year. It had a collection of police strobe lights he had rigged onto the car that he liked to use. He waited for Meghan outside the apartment complex.

"Where's our forensic kit?" she asked, seeing his hands were empty.

"I found the toolbox under the counter in storage," he explained. "I didn't know if you wanted that or not. I can go back and get it." His gloved thumb pointed behind him.

"Never mind," Meghan said with a sigh. She faced the ramp and they ascended through the main doors of the building. The foyer cut the first floor in half. Stairwells were at opposite ends of the building. Only one stairway had an exit to the side parking lot. It felt as if some fire code issues were being overlooked, but Meghan had more important things to worry about.

"Brian was pretty shaken up," Oliver said as he walked slightly behind Meghan along the first-floor corridor. Space was only ample enough for one and a half people walking together. "He said Nancy was supposed to be at work this morning."

"Where is Brian now?" Meghan reached into her parka, removed the leather-bound notebook she received from Mark before their divorce, before he got bored with their marriage, and started cheating on Meghan with the courtesy clerk in their neighborhood grocery store, three miles from the home they purchased together in New York. Meghan kept the notebook because it was more reliable than Mark in the long run.

"Him and Cheryl are in Nancy's apartment."

A rookie move, keeping suspects at the scene of the crime, but she kept her observation buttoned up tight. Once in the stairwell, Meghan felt they had a little more privacy. "Did Brian say how he found Nancy?"

"She was in her bedroom."

Meghan nodded. She'd meant to take the stairs two at a time. Only her winter boots were too heavy, and exercise for her since taking over the position happened about as often as she saw a butterfly. It was once, in July, a few years ago.

"Did you see what happened?"

"Naw, Lester said to keep out."

"That's good."

"He thought it was best to leave it for you to sort out."

They reached the second floor, and Meghan was out of breath, thighs burning. Oliver managed to get ahead of her. He had about a hundred pounds on her. She'd be damned, if he wasn't stopping, neither was she.

"When we get into the apartment, I want you to take Cheryl and Brian downstairs. Keep them together, and with you at all times. Don't let them so much as make a phone call until we get this sorted out."

"You know what happened to Nancy?" Oliver asked.

14

By the time they reached the third landing, he held open the door for her. Oliver had a round hairless face. Like most Inuit men, he had a thick mop of coal black hair on the top of his head with no middle-aged balding as it happened to men without the precious nectar of Native Alaskan blood flowing through their veins, with little to no facial hair. Oliver was missing a pinkie on his left hand. A harbor seal took it when he was seal hunting with his father years ago, a story he liked to tell the children whenever they visited the school during career days.

The renters on the third floor moved as directed back into their apartments before she made an appearance. At the far end of the hall, closest to the exit door where they should have come upstairs, Nancy McCormick's apartment door stood open. Lester and Brian stood in the hallway. Brian was looking worried, Lester was leaning against the doorjamb with a countenance of indifference.

Lester had a mustache he'd cultivated since his senior year of high school and wore it with pride. He gave a curt nod to Meghan as she approached. Once she got a look inside, she saw Cheryl Snyder sitting in one of the three chairs at a small round wooden table. She had a box of facial tissue in front of her, several wadded tissues on the tabletop, and as Meghan cringed without showing it, hands all over everything, contaminating the scene.

"Brian, Cheryl," Meghan started. She'd trained at the FBI Academy in Quantico, Virginia. She had field and classroom training that taught Meghan how to be tactful without being belligerent with potential suspects. "Lester is going to escort you both downstairs. Oliver is going with you."

Meghan had her hand on Cheryl's back, physical contact to direct her out of the chair, and out of the apartment. Once the couple was in the hallway, Meghan closed the door. She stood with her back to the front door, scanning the immediate area for signs of a struggle. The counters in the kitchenette were spotless. She heard the dishwasher chugging. Cheryl wanted to collect the wadded facial tissue she'd left on the table, but Meghan wanted her to leave the rubbish.

Suddenly it occurred to Meghan she was in charge of something that she'd trained for and secretly wanted to tackle ever since she saw female cops on a television show when she was a little girl. While it was terrible to think it took a murder to solve a homicide, Meghan knew she had nothing to do with Nancy McCormick's death. And if circumstances around the woman's demise had anything to do with something nefarious, Meghan was in the right place and had arrived at the right time to put justice on the trail.

The apartment was small, quaint, and quiet, aside from the chugging of the dishwasher and the hum of the refrigerator.

She reached into the inner pocket of her parka before shedding the outer layer. Like most interior buildings in Alaska, the room temperature was set around 75°F to 80°F all year long. She'd climbed three flights of stairs, was a little out of breath, a lot out of shape, and as she slipped on the medical gloves, Meghan felt she needed to get to the bedroom before anything else happened that she couldn't anticipate.

Chapter Four

Nancy McCormick was a popular woman in town. She grew up in Anchorage, Alaska and moved to Kinguyakkii with Cheryl as adolescents when their father took a job at Caribou Mine on the North Slope. The native corporation founded the lead and zinc mine and managed by the Northwest Arctic Borough. Handled in-state meant freelance companies had to contract with the locals and received fewer profits than typical trade agreements in the lower-forty-eight when companies raped the lands, harvested every last drop of natural goodness and paid the owners pennies on the dollar.

The McCormicks were well-to-do in Kinguyakkii, Nancy and Cheryl's father was a hands-on foreman at the mine who rose to VP of operations. He walked on a few people over the years before succumbing to lead poisoning from improper handling. Nancy was fourteen when she and Cheryl and their mother settled in the village while their father, Brad McCormick, left them for months at a time to manage the world's largest producer of zinc from the densest concentration of zinc reserves on the planet.

They had style and clout, and money until Brad died eight years ago, and then it all went south physically and emotionally. Cheryl and Nancy's mother beat feet out of the Town of Northern Lights before the body had cooled to tundra temperatures. She took the life insurance policy and vacated to Arizona to set up house in Mesa with Nancy tagging along. Cheryl had met Brian by the time their father died and opted to stay, eke out a living in town and start a life with her boyfriend, Brian.

One of the benefits of living in a small town, Meghan reasoned as she monitored the bedroom from

17

the doorway, personal histories from neighbors was bound to rub off after a spell.

***

Nancy lay in bed. Meghan had seen dead bodies before, not as many as some agents, few enough to feel that ticking in the back of her skull that warned her primal nerve that the woman lying in the queen-sized bed with the pretty floral duvet and feather pillows was dead not sleeping.

The room was reasonably orderly, in the way that a woman maintained it when they weren't expecting guests, or expecting a guest who didn't mind or care if there were clothes on the floor, the closet door was open, and Nancy hadn't finished putting away the folded clothes from the laundry basket on the small kitchen chair she had moved to her bedroom at some point.

The small prefabricated dresser to the right drew Meghan's attention. When she felt there wasn't any valuable evidence on the floor, she took delicate and deliberate steps toward the five-drawer dresser. On the surface was a collection of female trinkets. A large department store vanilla candle, three-quarters burned. Meghan picked it up with her gloved hand to look inside. The layer of dust over the wax told her the wick hadn't been lit recently. There was an ashtray on the dresser.

Mountain Manor was supposed to be smoke-free. By the heaps of cigarette butts all over the ground outside the complex suggested most renters followed the rules. Nancy didn't seem to care for the regulation. There was a scarf, wool hat, jewelry, a glove, and the ashtray with at least three different cigarette ends inside the bowl.

Meghan took the eight steps it took to reach the bedside from the dresser. The nightstand was cluttered, make-up, nail polish tubes, and the drawer was partially open. Meghan used one finger wedged inside to pull the drawer open enough to peer inside, revealing nothing out of the ordinary.

"Hello, Nancy," Meghan whispered to the woman lying in bed. Her face was exposed. Lester was right. A bluish and gray hue coated Nancy's skin. "My name's Meghan. Do you remember me? I used to come into the diner sometimes."

Meghan looked at the thin carpet under the bed. There was a multitude of fibers, some debris from lack of vacuuming regularly. There were no bottles of alcohol present. That was a good sign, possibly. It meant whatever happened between Nancy and the person who took the woman's life, wasn't fueled by bootlegged booze.

Kinguyakkii was a 'dry village.' In Alaska, there were three types of villages in the 'bush.' Many of the Alaskan communities were governed by elders who had seen the worst of subjugation. Between the Russian Orthodox explorers before the United States purchased the land, and the American settlers who ventured into Alaska seeking gold, in the same order as classifying the lower-forty-eight Native Americans. Native Alaskans had to endure the worst treatment for the sake of civilization. White settlers brought education and the whip, and a lot of booze with them.

Many of the oldest of the Alaska Natives still remembered how it was, usually more whip than education, while the alcohol flowed. By the time most of the Native Americans were run off the lands to the south, Alaskans were still an unruly people according to the government. Statehood happened at the beginning of 1959. There was an earlier generation in-state that saw the worst. Alcohol was a big part of the problem. Many of the interior and northern villages, places inaccessible by land or sea banned alcoholic beverages. Airlines did the rest. It was illegal to transport alcohol through the air without the permits.

While a Borough Council managed the town, the members were descendants of men and women tortured for the sake of fur trading, gold, and sovereignties of a people who lived in one place for thousands of years. Blood quantum went a long way in Alaska, Meghan knew alcohol-fueled problems and indigenous people were wise to its lethal power and continued to vote it out of the Town of Northern Lights.

"You're still a beautiful woman," Meghan said. She bent close, used an LED flashlight she carried in her jacket pocket at all times. It was standard equipment in a place where it was dark months out of the year. Even Nancy's bedroom, with the lights on, still held deep shadows that needed cutting with the flashlight.

"What was that?" Lester stood at the bedroom door.

Meghan stood up straight, pocketed the flashlight. Rather than explain to Lester that she sometimes had a habit of talking to the dead because, well, Meghan thought since she was about to get intimately involved in their lives, dig in the dirt and find out why and how they died, it would be a good idea to get past the greetings.

"Do we have a medical examiner in town, Lester?" It was one of the many questions she still hadn't asked because most of the time she had to wait

20

until something happened before the right item came along.

"We got Eric." The quip described a 'thing' rather than a 'who.'

It wasn't meant to be a loaded question, but sometimes Lester assumed when someone spoke with him, they already knew the outcome. "Remind me again who Eric is?" Meghan rubbed her forehead with her wrist.

"He's the manager at the trader store."

"Is he a licensed medical doctor?" While it wasn't impossible to think a doctor worked at an Alaska Native trading company, it was best to second guess. She'd seen some exciting things since moving to the largest state in the Union. Anything, and everything was possible.

"Well, he gets called by the clinic to help take bodies out of their homes if someone dies."

"So, he's a coroner." Meghan nodded.

Lester shrugged. "If you say so," it came out not as an insult, more like an added layer of what made up a man like Eric.

"Give him a call, see if he can come over. We'll need him later."

"Sure thing, Chief."

Suddenly Oliver came into view. He was a few years younger than Lester; he looked a little pale peaking over the man's shoulder into the room.

"Who's watching to make sure no one is coming upstairs?" she asked her only two officers.

They needed more help, but the city's budget was managed by a miser who scrutinized and questioned all expenditures by the town police. Fuel for the chief of police Chevy Suburban wasn't part of the budget, so Meghan filled the gas tank sparingly. Fuel in the village was as precious as gold or silver, priced anywhere between three to five times more per gallon than any of the cities on the road system. More officers weren't part of the annual financial plan, and neither was fuel for a gas-guzzling rusty beast.

Oliver pointed back the way he came. "I locked the door."

"Okay."

Meghan stepped away from the bed, retracing the steps she took to reach the body. "Lester, you touch Nancy with your bare hand?"

"I saw her from the doorway," he explained. "I knew she was dead, but, yeah, I checked for a pulse at her wrist."

"Okay, good."

"I screamed too," he added with a shrug.

"To see if she woke up?"

"Yeah, sure," he said. "Okay."

"Get the camera and start taking pictures everywhere—what are you doing?"

Oliver and Lester both had out their smartphones. A flash went off on Oliver's phone before he stopped taking pictures.

"You can't take pictures with your phones, gentlemen. Go get the camera at the police station."

"We have a camera?" Oliver asked.

"Don't we?"

22

"Never needed one," Lester said. He held up his smartphone. "I take pictures with my phone for DV calls."

"We can't use phones for pictures here. Do you know anyone in town that has a digital camera?"

"Sure, Calvin has a nice camera."

"Calvin Everett?" she clarified.

"Yeah, he's got a real nice camera."

"You know he's a reporter, right?" Meghan asked. "We can't have a reporter for the *Northern Lights Sounder* come into a crime scene and take pictures."

"I'm sure if you asked him, he'd do it." Oliver tucked away his phone. Both men stood respectfully outside the bedroom door. "He's outside."

Meghan crossed the room and went into the small hall. News got out, traveled faster than the internet around town. Someone said something, by now everyone in town who had access to anyone else knew what was going on inside Mountain Manor.

In the kitchen, Meghan took charge and dished out the orders. "Lester, head to the airport. See if anyone flew out of here last night. Talk to each of the charter pilots and the cargo pilots. See if you can get a passenger manifest from them if they had scheduled or unscheduled flights."

She turned to Oliver. "I need you to contain this floor. If anyone who doesn't belong on this floor is here, get them out of here. I don't want anyone near this apartment. We don't have a forensic kit?"

Both men shook their heads.

23

"Okay," she said with a sigh. "Oliver, stand outside the door. I'll be right back."

Meghan and Lester moved down the stairwell closest to Nancy's door. Oliver stood in the hallway. He started talking to the neighbors nearest to Nancy's apartment the moment Meghan was in the hall. She made a mental note to go over how they needed to handle a situation if something like this happened again. She'd left the FBI and the real world to get anyway from this sort of crisis.

Now she was at the top of the world, stepping out into the March winds, looking at the gray sky. Snow clung to any part of the ground that didn't get a touch of sunlight. There was no such thing as spring in Alaska. It went from deep winter to a few weeks of summer and back to winter again. Sometimes summer came and went when Meghan was taking a long hot bath in her rental. It was murder, and while Meghan knew all about how to manage an active case, she felt there were tripwires in the dregs of snow that crunched underfoot.

Chapter Five

Calvin Everett was an attractive man in his fifties. There was no denying that he had a certain charm about him. The moment he saw Meghan emerge from Mountain Manor, he gave a wave and a smile. She didn't have anything official to say to him, but necessity and the fact that he managed to keep himself fit when there wasn't much to do in town except hang out with friends, watch movies, and order pizza from the one pizza delivery place in five hundred miles, made her gravitate toward him.

"Can I talk to you a minute?" Meghan asked. Calvin stood with Brian and Cheryl Snyder. The couple was at their truck, waiting. Cheryl's eyes were puffy and red. Brian consoled his wife as best he could. Meghan needed to talk to them, but Nancy took precedence.

"Is it true?" Calvin asked. He had a digital recorder hovering in front of Meghan's mouth.

She cleared her throat and moved toward the police rig. The Chevy Suburban was due for retirement. It burned gas, leaked oil. It was twenty years old, and for a town that was only roughly thirty miles square, the Suburban had over 150,000 miles on the odometer. That was a lot of trips around town.

"I can't comment on an ongoing investigation," she answered.

Calvin was taken aback by the answer. He stood near as Meghan pulled open the rear hatch on the truck and then let the gate drop. The collecting of detritus in the rear was as many generations old as the truck. She searched through the various cardboard boxes.

"Is Nancy dead?" he whispered.

She frowned at him and shook her head. "Can I do my job so you can have all the dirt you want to sling and make my department, or the town look bad?"

Calvin stopped the recorder. He dropped it into his coat pocket. "You think this is a scoop for me?"

"Well, the camera around your neck, the digital recorder, the fact you went and spoke to the victim's family," she said. "Yeah, I think this is your big scoop."

"Listen, I know you've been avoiding me since you got here."

Meghan didn't find what she wanted in the back, slammed the rear gate and hatch. She moved to the side of the truck and opened the rear door to search in the boxes on the floorboards. "I get you to want to do a puff piece on me for your devoted readers."

"You got me all wrong," Calvin mumbled. Meghan saw how he bristled at the observation. He took a few steps back from her. When he turned away, Meghan called to him.

More people began to pull into the parking lot at the apartment complex. Since there were no designated lines for parking, only a flat gravel surface, void of grass, most the area around Mountain Manor was designated parking.

"Listen, Calvin. You want to do me a favor?"

He looked innocent. He had short salt and pepper hair, a week's worth of beard on his chin that matched the flavor on his head. He didn't wear a hat for the morning, and he looked as if, like Meghan, he slept in the clothes he wore to the scene.

26

"Can I rent your camera?"

Instinctively, his hands went to the excellent digital camera hanging from the strap at his neck. It had a 200mm lens on it, and there was a camera bag on his shoulder. Meghan approached him. She'd found two full boxes of wooden matches and a roll of clear packing tape and carried them with her. Calvin was a few inches taller than Meghan, a height she liked in men. Not too tall she'd have to stand on tiptoes to kiss him.

The idea dropped out of her head when she coughed with embarrassment at the thought. "I just really want to buy your memory card in the camera. The department doesn't have a budget for a digital camera—"

"That's fine," he said, relinquishing the camera without an argument. "Consider it a professional courtesy." He handed Meghan the camera. "And for your record, Brian and I go way back. I've known him for years. I know Cheryl, and I know—knew Nancy." He turned from her and wandered back to where Nancy's family waited, grieving in the truck.

Meghan needed to focus. Before she left the truck, Meghan fished around inside her purse on the passenger seat of the police truck and removed the makeup brush she had but never found the time to use. She shook away the idea that she'd underestimated Calvin, put the camera strap around her neck, and went back into the building. Oliver followed his boss into the apartment complex.

Chapter Six

Since the small kitchen table had been compromised by Brian and Cheryl when they arrived, Meghan used the place as a point of her operation. She put down her collection of items, including the digital camera. Then she searched the cupboards in the kitchenette until she found what she wanted. Oliver stood with his back to the door, watching Meghan work.

She'd removed the parka earlier upon arrival, now Meghan took off the hooded sweatshirt she wore underneath the winter outerwear. One thing Meghan learned from day one in Alaska, the only way to keep warm was all about the layers of clothing.

"What are you doing, Chief?"

Meghan sat at the table. She had the entire ingredient list and a mixing bowl. "You ever watch those cop shows on TV?"

"Yeah, you mean the British ones where old people or town priests solved crimes?"

"No, I'm talking about the American shows where pretty people wear designer clothes, drive expensive cars, and have places to work where there are architectural dreams and next to no lighting?"

"Oh yeah," Oliver said and laughed.

Meghan winked at him. "If this was a TV show, this is where they'd start the stylized editing, nifty camera work, and have the popular music playing for a montage."

She picked up the digital camera and handed it to Oliver carefully. "You know how to use this?"

"Sure."

"Please be careful with it. I want you to take pictures of everything, everything in the kitchen, here at the table, in the living room, bathroom, all around except the bedroom. I'll photograph the bedroom."

"Okay, I can do that. What are you making?"

Meghan began lighting the stick matches and dropping them into the glass mixing bowl as they burned to the stub ends.

"We don't have a fingerprint kit. You can make homemade fingerprint powder with carbon from the wooden matches, mixed with this," she said and held up the box of corn starch. "Put these two ingredients together, mix well, and we have fingerprint powder." She glanced to Oliver's bare hands. "Make sure you don't touch anything. Just take pictures."

***

Over the next hour, while Oliver took pictures, Meghan began dusting surfaces with the makeshift fingerprint powder. It had a grainy consistency and a few times she had to dig out splinters of wood. After the fifth dusting and collecting the print with the strips of packing tape, Meghan had a system that worked. Each place she took prints, she labeled with a marker found in a junk drawer in the kitchen.

She hit the main areas that seemed relevant. Considering Nancy had company, the person who took her life. The fact there was no forced entry, that none of her neighbors complained about hearing a verbal dispute, meant Nancy knew her killer.

Meghan dusted the surfaces in the kitchen, the refrigerator handle, and the handle to the pantry. She dusted the bathroom. The facet handles, the shower knobs, the toilet handle, and the toilet seat. Meghan fingerprinted the doorknobs in the apartment, the

29

coffee table surface. There was an ashtray with what looked like three different kinds of cigarette butts. Since she wasn't a smoker, she'd have to check the brands.

By the time she finished fingerprinting the dresser, nightstand, and the closet doorknob, Oliver stood quietly in the doorway.

"You okay?" she asked. There were strips of packing tape in stacks on the floor. Everywhere she made a print set, Meghan labeled and placed them in piles on the floor.

"Yeah," he replied quietly. "I ain't never seen a dead person 'cept my Gram, but I was really young when she died."

Meghan took the digital camera from Oliver. "It's not easy, I know. How well did you know Nancy?"

"Oh, you know. From the diner," he said, suppressing a smile. "I go sometimes, and she was there."

"She's a pretty girl."

"Yeah." He looked somber. "She was."

Meghan frowned, glancing around the bedside table. "Did you see her cell phone anywhere?"

"No."

"I'm going to finish taking pictures in the bedroom. Collect the fingerprint samples. I've numbered all of them, so you don't have to worry about mixing them up." Meghan rolled her wavy copper hair over her ear as she looked at Oliver. "Listen, this is the time that I need you to be is a sworn police officer. Do you understand? You can't talk to anyone out there about this. We need to find

30

out everything we can. I'll call the Alaska State Troopers as soon as I'm done interviewing Cheryl and Brian. We'll get a list of people to talk to later. Right now, I want to preserve the rest of the evidence. Go downstairs, see if the coroner is here. We'll move her as soon as I take some pictures and examine her more. You don't need to stick around for that, okay?"

Meghan touched Oliver's shoulder.

"Sure, Boss, I'll take care of it."

When Oliver collected the fingerprint tapes and left Meghan alone in the apartment, she took the rest of the photographs in the bedroom. After photos of Nancy's body on the bed with the sheet where it was, Meghan sighed.

"I'm sorry, Nancy," she whispered respectfully. Carefully, Meghan rolled back the duvet and folded it into squares. She did the same for the bed sheet. "I have to look, you know?"

Nancy wore a simple extra-large T-shirt to bed, and a pair of sweatpants, with socks.

"So, you were either expecting your company to leave when you went to bed. Or you weren't in the mood last night." Considering that Nancy still wore sweatpants and socks told Meghan that she likely hadn't been sexually assaulted before the murder.

She leaned over Nancy. The woman lay on her stomach, faced the dresser and nightstand. There were bruises on her neck. Taking fingerprints from the skin was tricky with regular dust; the homemade powder was out of the question. When Meghan shipped the body back to Anchorage for an autopsy, she didn't want a pathologist wondering why the corpse smelled like burnt matches and corn starch.

31

Once Meghan collected all the photographic evidence she needed, she stood in the bedroom for a few minutes. Silently, she gave the woman a respectful, mourning moment. Before she left the apartment, Meghan double-checked under the bed, in case the killer left a calling card.

Satisfied she hadn't missed anything; Meghan left the apartment to finish with the witnesses and get ready for the rest of her investigation.

Chapter Seven

It was after four in the afternoon. Meghan had a headache she chalked up to stress and the fact she'd missed out on coffee. Once she collected the memory card from the digital camera, she carefully handed it back to Calvin.

"Thank you."

"You got me all wrong," was all he said and left the area where most of the village had turned out to watch the show.

It was getting dark already. She'd burned up the meager daylight inside Nancy's apartment. Now she had to coordinate the rest of the business.

"What's next, Boss?" Oliver addressed her as his superior without malice. It was a term of hierarchy and nothing more. They were police officers before Meghan arrived to take over as chief of police, neither Olive nor Lester wanted the job, content with their roles as peace officers without the added drama that came with the title she bore.

"Can you and Lester help Eric move the body?"

Eric Kennedy, still wearing the work smock he wore at the trader store under the heavy jacket. There was black beaver fur hat on his head, a coveted head cover that was hot in the coldest of temperatures. Meghan stuck to the synthetic headgear and coats. Some of the Inuit people wore seal skin boots, fur-lined kuspuks—traditional hooded overshirts, and fur-lined mittens. Much of the traditional clothing was still heavily sought after in 'bush' Alaska. Native Alaskans were handy with needle and thread.

Since Eric ran the local trading post, he got the first choice of pedaled furs when the hunters brought them to town as long as the animals were in season and not protected species.

"Can you transport her to the clinic?" Meghan asked.

"I can," Eric said. "But why am I taking her to the clinic?"

"We need to keep her in the morgue."

"There's not a morgue at the clinic, Chief," Lester added. "Any time we have to hold a body, Eric takes it back to the store with him."

Eric grinned. "I cleared out some space in the walk-in cooler. She'll be fine there."

Meghan did her best not to shake her head. "Okay. Can you at least lock the cooler?"

"Sure can."

"Are you transporting her in that?"

Summer was a flash in the midnight sun. Eric knew how to take advantage of most business he had in town. He had the only van in town. It was a white Chevy van with murals of ice cream painted on the sides. For the few weeks, it was warm enough to drive through town, he blared music from the van, and village kids came from every corner of the little town to purchase ice cream cones and popsicle sticks. Nancy was about to be transported to the trading post cooler in the back of an ice cream truck.

"Sure, why not?" Eric didn't seem bothered by it any more than Lester.

She waved them away and went to where Brian paced in front of the truck. "I'm sorry it took so long."

"Cheryl went back home," he said. "I thought I should stay."

"Thank you." Meghan glanced around the area. People were staring at them — many of the closest groups hushed when she arrived to talk to Brian. "We should head to your house. We can talk there."

"Okay."

Before Meghan turned to get to the police truck, she asked, "Do you or Cheryl have Nancy's cell phone?"

He shook his head.

She took out her smartphone, opened the dialer, and handed it to Brian. "Just type in Nancy's number, don't hit 'dial,' thanks."

In the police truck, waiting a few minutes for the engine to warm up, the heater to work, Meghan held her breath and connected the number Brian put into her phone. Instead of going directly to voicemail, the phone rang six times until Nancy's cheery voice came on and asked the caller to leave a message. The killer took Nancy's phone. It wasn't anywhere in the apartment; Meghan was sure of that. It was still on, wherever it was, and made her think that when she called Nancy's phone, the killer heard it ringing.

Chapter Eight

The Town of Northern Lights had roughly three thousand residents in the immediate area. That was one thousand people for each of the police officers in town. During the winter, when the rivers and Kinguyakkii Bay froze solid, people came to town riding four-wheelers and snowmobiles. That meant more business for Kinguyakkii Police Department.

There were fistfights outside the bingo hall on Friday and Saturday nights. Sometimes the occasional squabble from a lovers' triangle. If they were fortunate, when the mood struck, sometimes bootleggers brought a batch of booze into town. That ramped up the fights and added drunk driving to the mix.

They were meant to keep the peace. Since the North Slope Borough Council made the rules, Meghan had to follow them. She took the job as the Chief of Police for the town with the understanding that she was hired to do all the things those police officers did in the lower-forty-eight except she wasn't issued a firearm. As Village Public Safety Officers, or VPSOs, had the power to arrest, even had handcuffs, but weapons were out of the question.

She had pepper spray. Lester and Oliver had pepper spray and handcuffs. They'd been certified to use the small canisters, but mostly the deterrents were for show and dare because Oliver sometimes sprayed caribou steaks with his pepper spray on the barbeque grill before he ate them.

When people from outlining villages came to town, most of them were armed. Everyone carried a gun in the wild. The environment was harsh and dangerous. Sometimes the occasional polar bear wandered into town. It was one of the very few animals on the planet that actively hunted, killed, and ate people. Polar bears weren't picky about their food.

Meghan had to do it all without a gun and only had the occasional sharp sarcasm to wield when she came face to face with danger. People fought; it was human nature. Meghan accepted the job as chief because the town had its share of bumps but never murder. There was one unsolved homicide on the books, and that was years before she arrived.

***

Brian and Cheryl lived in a small two-bedroom house on Bison Street. It was five houses down from the house Meghan rented. She knew the couple from the diner, one of the three places in town to eat. Other than the pizza place, there was a Chinese restaurant operated by a pleasant Latino couple, Miguel and Leticia Rodriguez, who managed to incorporate a collection of traditional Mexican dishes. Midnight Sun Café was a greasy diner, bacon and eggs in the morning, French fries and steaks in the night. Meghan ruled out competition between the restaurants as a motive because each of the businesses balanced their menus not out to do or interfere with other restaurateurs.

They had a ten-year-old child who had lost his aunt and didn't understand what was going on when Meghan visited the house. The Snyders sent the little boy to his room to play video games while they had a conversation with the police chief.

"Coffee?" Brian offered.

"Oh, God, yes, please." Greedily, Meghan accepted the steaming cup. Cheryl put a collection of flavored creamer and sugar on the dinner table, done in a way that was practiced without thought. "That's so good," she said after the first sip. "Thank you."

"Can you tell us what happened?" Cheryl sat across from Meghan. Brian stood behind her, hand on her shoulder.

Meghan tried not to think about him not sitting beside his wife, tried not working out that he stood in the way that kept him from facing his wife, and his left hand tucked into his pants pocket as if the wedding band was a problem. She didn't want to think about that. It was the sort of observation that got her into trouble sometimes as an FBI agent.

"Tell me a little about the last time you saw Nancy."

The breath caught in Cheryl's throat; Brian answered for the two of them. "She left work early Saturday. Normally she closes."

"Did she have a date?"

"Nancy didn't believe in dating," Cheryl said with some venom on the words. Rather than squeeze out more details, Meghan waited. Sometimes people worked out they said things that could be considered suspicious and gave follow-up details to clarify the statement. "After her divorce, Nancy wanted to live her life on her own terms."

"I wouldn't go that far," Brian added. "She came back here broke and never managed her money very well."

"I noticed an aluminum Christmas cookie tin on the refrigerator," Meghan pointed out. "It was empty."

Cheryl nodded. "Nancy kept her tips from waitressing in that container."

"I dusted it for fingerprints. I want to collect your fingerprints too before I leave. So that I can eliminate them from the apartment."

"I thought the Alaska State Troopers are going to handle the investigation." There was a worried look passing over his face, or perhaps Meghan was just too tired to read clearly. She glimpsed Brian rubbing his fingertips on his pants.

"They will, likely. For now, I want to get the preliminary interviews done so we don't have to bother you again." She turned the coffee mug in her hands. "Do you know who Nancy was seeing?"

Brian shook his head, looking away from Meghan. Cheryl pursed her lips. "She was very popular. I think Nancy peaked in high school." It wasn't animosity; their sibling relationship was a mystery to anyone looking in on them. Like most sisters, they had a dialogue between them that outsiders might consider rude or cruel.

While Meghan felt it was a little bitter to talk about her sister negatively, grieving was a fickle thing, no two people grieved the same way, and there were so many levels, anger and jealousy happened sometimes, and Meghan didn't want to read too much into it.

"It was rough sometimes. All the boys wanted her; all the girls wanted to be like her. When we got older, when she decided to get married, I felt like she was just doing it because Brian and I were married and happy. Marriage for Nancy never worked out because she turned into the kind of woman who took husbands away from wives."

There was some real dirty laundry that needed airing out, Meghan considered. It wasn't going to help

39

her figure out who killed Cheryl's sister unless some of the dirty shirts or underwear had names written in the collar or waistbands. She finished the coffee, asked Brian and Cheryl to make themselves available if she needed to speak to them again.

Chapter Nine

Meghan returned to the police station feeling heavy, burdened by the responsibility of investigating a murder without the proper equipment or personnel, and the layers of outwear Meghan shed as soon as she unlocked the door.

Kinguyakkii Police Department was a name more than a permanent building. Oliver and Lester took turns, answering phone calls to the department. The town didn't have a 911 dispatcher or funding for a call center, but they had Oliver and Lester, who knew everyone in and around town. Most of the calls to the department were handled over the phone, sometimes with follow-up if there was theft or damages involved.

Lester sometimes let his wife answer police department calls when he was on-duty. Silvia Graves had a direct approach to most calls, fielding insults, and punting accusations at the callers, sometimes getting feuding couples on the phone together and conduct a relationship intervention right then. For all the quirkiness of the town, it worked.

There were two modular contractor trailers put together that made up the physical building of the police station. Like most of the buildings, even the temporary ones in Kinguyakkii were aboveground structures. Digging into the tundra wasn't how to make structures stable.

Even the hotel and Mountain Manor, two of the most significant buildings in the village, were constructed on top of the tundra, icy slurry that had a temperament of molasses when the weather warmed up. Larger structures needed the ground frozen to keep from pulling apart the building at the seams. Long steel poles surrounded the buildings, driven deep

41

into the tundra to keep the land stable. Sealed refrigerant moves down when the weather gets too warm up top, and up when the ground is frozen.

After construction, the contractors leave behind most of the leftover building materials, including the contractor trailers. Wisely, years ago, someone from town thought it was a good idea to have two of the contractor trailers welded together and placed next door to the town hall.

Meghan's office was used for storage when she first arrived. It was the only place inside the building, other than the tiny bathroom, that had a door. Claiming the room as office space meant to shift around the years of accumulated files and boxes that had no relevance to policing and needed to go away entirely.

Once out of the cold weather gear, Meghan rounded the desk to boot up the laptop, her personal computer since the town was too stingy to spring for a department computer. Meghan fished the memory card from her pants pocket and slipped it into the laptop.

Oliver had an eye for detail. He took hundreds of photographs and knew what looked important. She liked what he saw through the camera lens.

"What the hell is going on!"

Meghan jumped in her seat and looked up at the man staring at her from the doorway of her office. She'd locked the outer door to the station. Lester was still collecting information on flights leaving town. Since it was after five in the evening, Silvia probably called him home again for dinner.

Oliver volunteered to patrol the town since Meghan was tied up with the investigation. Nancy's body was safely tucked away at the trading post store, and she hadn't had a moment to herself all day.

Duane Warren was the mayor of Kinguyakkii. He wore the title 'Mayor' on every piece of outerwear, sweatshirt, and t-shirt he owned. While they had no budget for simple things like paper or pens, somehow the town hall had money in the budget for embroidery.

"You scared the shit out of me!" Meghan recovered, straightened in her chair and went back to the laptop screen.

"What are you doing?" he asked.

Rumor had it that Duane grew up in Seattle, earned a law degree, and through the course of impractical means, was eventually disbarred and disgraced, and escaped to Alaska, using his limited imagination to run the Town of Northern Lights into the ground while no one was looking.

"I'm doing my job." She concentrated on the image files, making folders, and filing them accordingly. She glanced up at him. "What did you need?"

"You're not supposed to be investigating a murder. That's a job for the troopers."

"I'm gathering all the preliminary evidence, Duane. They'll thank me for the extra work."

"Did you even call them?" Duane was somewhere between forty and sixty years of age. There was something about living inside the Arctic Circle that made it hard to gauge ages on a glance. Trees didn't grow in the Arctic because the root system needed deep soil to stand firm. Lichen, grass, herbs, and shrubs grew in clusters, close to the ground to protect plants against cold winds. Deeper into the field was supposed to be frozen. It made it hard to make basements, trees to grow, and bury the dead. Somehow, living in crisp air made people age differently than in the real world.

"I'm going to call them in a while. I want to get my report written up and send it to them."

"That's not how we do things around here." He stood with fists on his hips as if scolding Meghan. She failed to be intimidated by him.

"Look, Duane, do I come over to town hall to tell you how to do your job?"

"Yes, as a matter of fact, you do."

"Well, that's because you never have enough budget for the police department. Other than that, you do whatever it is you do there, and I suggest you let me do my job."

"You know, I'm a lawyer, I know what you're supposed to be doing. You're not supposed to be investigating a murder by yourself."

Meghan refused to stoop lower than Duane when it came to dishing out insults. So far, he was moderately civil. She stood up. While she wanted to point out to him that he'd been disbarred, it wouldn't get anything accomplished, only make him bitterer.

Instead, she walked around the desk, pulled at the hem of her sweater, conscious of her hips, and walked toward him. She wasn't very tall. Tall enough for the FBI and that's all that mattered at one time. But like most of the mountain men in town, burly, broad shoulders, bearded, Duane practically towered over her.

"I would appreciate it if you didn't sneak into the station. I locked the door. You have a key—"

"I'm the mayor—"

"I'm the Chief of Police. This is my place of business. I don't have a key to town hall, Duane. I would appreciate if you went back to your office, and I will return to mine." She managed to back him out the office door and closed it between them.

Meghan returned to the desk. She couldn't see Duane hovering outside the door, but she knew he didn't have a key to her office. "You need to call the trooper, Sheppard!" The thin door muted his voice.

"Thank you, Duane. Goodnight." Meghan sighed and continued to organize the images. There was a ticking in her head that was exasperated by the sudden and unexpected appearance of Duane. It was hours since the discovery of the body. She had jurisdiction in town and the surrounding villages because there was never enough Alaskan State Troopers to go around. She wasn't elected as a county sheriff; Meghan was hired to do the job. Meghan wasn't dictated to do anything that didn't fit her idea of what was her job.

Anchorage was the seat of the Alaska State Troopers. There was a designated telephone number to call. Once she reached someone, after what felt like ten minutes of automated prompts, the person on the phone sounded more annoyed than worried about the reason she called.

"So, the infamous Meghan Sheppard," he addressed her.

"Well, now, that's no way to start a conversation, Detective."

He'd come on the line after a five-minute hold filled with terrible jazz melodies. Gregory Anderson was the name he gave as soon as he came on the line. Meghan took a moment to throw 'Detective Gregory Anderson' in the search bar on the internet to see what came back at her. He was a little overweight according to the few photos that popped up. She'd never heard of him before; clearly, he knew Meghan through police channels. Anderson was one of the five violent crime detectives with the State Troopers.

"You got yourself a murder I hear."

It took her by surprise. "How do you know already?"

"We got little birds in town."

"By little birds you mean anyone with a phone and an ear to the crowd?"

"That works," he mumbled indifferently.

"I'm finishing up the preliminary report and can email it to you in an hour or so."

"That works. You get some pictures too?"

"I did."

"We've flagged all the flights from your area of the woods."

"I had one of my officers collect passenger manifests from the outgoing flights since Friday night."

"Anyone leaving by boat?" he asked.

"We've got break up happening right now."

"It's a little early for break up."

"Well, times are changing." Ice on the river and bay made stable travel avenue when it was solid. An inch of ice could hold a lot of weight. Four inches thick was suitable for walking, skating, and fast machines like four-wheelers or snowmobiles. Thicker ice meant heavier vehicles. Cars, trucks, sometimes heavy operation equipment were driven downriver from town during cold weather.

Now with break up, icy was iffy and not stable. Those slabs of ice dropped in a second, once the water started moving again, it hauled tons of ice out to the bay. Ice was dangerous and unpredictable. When it was free-flowing, no one could drive on it, and the rivers were too dangerous to navigate boats because hulls would be shredded.

"So, no boats and no one is stupid enough to drive out of town." Detective Anderson was aware of the logistics of living in 'bush Alaska,' the only way out of town that time of year was by plane. His comment suggested Anderson had no patience for villagers. Most people who didn't understand the balance of living in rural Alaska thought most people in villages were hillbillies or hiding out. Meghan was neither of those, plus, she respected the Native Alaskans who refused to bend to the whims of ethnology that didn't impact them directly.

"You got a one-off thing." He still seemed bored by the event. "What happened to her?"

"I see you're already up on who and what, just not the how?"

"If I had to guess, your victim was either beaten to death or strangled."

"Nancy McCormick was strangled." She looked at the scribbling in her notebook. "I got an ex-husband named Peter McCormick. I think he either lives in Anchorage or Arizona. I'm not sure which." It was essential to have empathy for the job; many people who dealt with death daily became jaded. Meghan liked keeping in mind that she was solving a crime against a person, someone who lived and breathed, and not just the shell or a case number. Anderson threw around 'victim' like Nancy was just another statistic.

"I'll see if we can find out where he was at the time of the incident."

"Her sister mentioned that their relationship was a little strained. I'm pretty sure he's not in town."

"You got any leads?"

"She worked as a waitress for her sister and brother in-law's restaurant. Nancy kept tip money in a cookie tin on her fridge. The money's gone. I have tons of fingerprints. I'll eliminate the family, or at least put them into perspective."

"Sounds like you got a handle on it on your end. Where's the body?"

"For now, our coroner has it stored in the cooler at the trading post."

Anderson chuckled. "You mean Eric Kennedy?"

"Yeah, anything I should know about him?"

"Not really, he fancies himself an amateur pathologist. Once performed an autopsy on a village elder at the request of the family."

"He's not a licensed doctor, right?"

"Nope, but no one pressed charges either. Your predecessor was a bit of a coot, and things were a little backward then. It's still a good story to tell."

"I'll pass." She waited a while, listening to the rattle of the floorboard heater in the office. Anderson shuffled papers on the other end of the line.

"You send what you got for evidence; I'll have the detective in charge of that area contact you sometime tomorrow. You got a one-off."

"You keep saying that."

"You've been in Kinguyakkii long enough to know how it works there. The last murder was twenty years ago." Anderson pronounced it 'King-U-Aki-Aki,' and it wasn't half bad except he left out one of the syllables.

"That murder is still unsolved, by the way. And it's been fifteen years."

Anderson didn't bite at the facts. "Someone will eventually start talking. Once that happens, hook him up, and we'll be by to pick him up."

"You're thinking it's a man?"

He laughed because Meghan had a reputation and it spread all the way to Anchorage. "You already know the answer, Sheppard. Finish up what you've got, send it, and enjoy the rest of your night." He ended the call with an abrupt 'goodbye' and Meghan went through the motion of writing a report on the murder for the detective.

Chapter Ten

When the smartphone rang on the desk, Meghan didn't recognize the phone number. "This is Chief Sheppard."

"Hey, Meg—Chief Sheppard, this is Calvin Everett—"

"I am not at liberty to talk about an on-going investigation."

"This isn't about that," he said hurriedly, hoping to get in the information before she ended the call. "I'm calling because I saw the light on in the office. I wanted to check on you."

"I'm still working, Mr. Everett. That's what police officers do when there's been a crime. We continue to do our jobs."

"It's Calvin, Chief Sheppard. Just Calvin," he said with a sigh. "I know you don't trust me. I get it, I'm a reporter, and you're a cop. Our relationship is supposed to be tumultuous, and sometimes at odds, it's kind of cliché actually. I'm just a guy that does a job, and people appreciate what I do. They appreciate what you do too."

"Doesn't feel like it," she admitted.

"That's because you never let anyone in. Since you took the job, you don't share anything with anyone."

"I know there's a cool little thing on the computer you can type my name into and get all sorts of torrid information."

"I'm not talking about that. You make yourself unavailable to the community, and when they need you, you want to make sure they can reach out to you."

"Is that why you're calling me? To reach out to me?"

"It is, and I'm extending a hand in trust. Also, I noticed you hadn't eaten anything today."

Meghan frowned. "How would you know that?"

"Look to your left."

Meghan glanced to her left shoulder. While the trailers were elevated, the small window in the office showed the barren field on the east side of the building. Calvin sat behind the wheel of his little lime green Ford Focus. Vehicles that came to villages in rural Alaska rarely escaped. People used cars and trucks, sold them to others when they could move on. Calvin was the fifth or seventh owner of the Ford much in the way the police Suburban started as the school bus thirty years ago and evolved into something else.

He sat waving at her with the dome light. "I brought dinner. Are you in the mood for Chinese takeout?"

***

Relenting to an empty stomach, Meghan unlocked the door and let Calvin in. He had showered, shaved, and smelled of aftershave. Meghan ignored him the best she could and led him through the small swinging door that separated the front counter from the rest of police operations.

There was enough room for a sizeable Formica table and a collection of mismatched office chairs. Calvin put out the paper bags he brought. Meghan grabbed the stack of paper plates and napkins.

51

"I should probably pay you for the food." She sat at the table, stomach growling.

"Consider it a peace offering." Calvin went through the bags and held up containers. "We've got egg rolls, churros, fried rice, refried beans, soft tacos, and spicy chicken." He grinned. "Take your pick."

"Is there anywhere else on the planet where we have traditional Chinese and Authentic Mexican food at the same place?" She collected a smattering of each dish and an egg roll and was unable to pass on the churro.

They ate quietly together, facing each other across the full warped table. He had questions; she saw it on his face, the small lines at the corner of his eyes from squinting staring across snow when it was sunny. Sunlight reflecting off the snow was serious business in the north. At least, most of the thick snow had already melted away, leaving the mud, muck, and rutty ground.

"I want to confess something," he started.

Rather than coach him, Meghan waited, taking small bites while in the company of men because it was something her mother taught her as proper etiquette. Alone she'd devoured all of it within a few minutes. Now she had to look presentable, respectable. Eventually, she'd fill that void in her stomach.

"My camera has a redundant memory." He made a face with the confession. Grimaced as if expecting her to slap him or throw food in his face. The food was too good to waste, and he was too far away to reach. "Everything that goes to the memory card is just back-up from the camera memory."

"So, you have every shot of the crime scene."

52

"No, well, yes, I did. But I wanted you to know that I deleted them. All of them."

"Not before downloading and looking at them." She took her time, sipped on a soda from the small refrigerator in the department. Stocked by Lester, Oliver, and herself, they shared leftovers and kept it stocked with caffeinated drinks.

"Well, no. Okay, yes." He looked crestfallen. "I know, I know. But it's human nature, you know? I swear I deleted the pictures. All of them."

"Okay," she said quietly. "I have to take your word for it."

"You're mad at me," he pointed out.

"A little, yeah, I guess."

"I know. I'm sorry."

"It's not your fault. This department should have its own cameras. I'm grateful for you saving the day." She looked at the containers of food in front of them. "Twice today." Meghan wiped her mouth with a napkin and suppressed a belch.

"What happened to her?" he asked. It wasn't a reporter trying to get information out of a cop for a scoop in the paper. It was a man asking someone who knew what was going on when the tragedy happened.

"How well did you know Nancy?"

"Well," he started and smiled. "She was very, very popular."

Meghan nodded. "Her sister said the same thing."

"I think Nancy liked all the boys chasing her."

"Did you ever chase her?"

He waited to answer. Nancy was thirty-three, still holding on the youthful twenty-six appearance. It was the magic of a woman to have the right form-fitting underwear, the sense of the proper application of make-up, and the right lighting to pull off the magnetism and allure. "I chased briefly. Shortly after her divorce, we started to get to know each other. Small acquaintance through the diner," he added. "I think she came back to Kinguyakkii only because her sister had a business that could use Nancy."

Meghan smiled because Calvin pronounced the Inuit word like a lifelong Alaskan with all five syllables rolling off his talented tongue.

"What happened?"

"I saw through her. Honestly, I really wasn't interested in dating Nancy. She was new in town. You know how it is."

"Not really," Meghan said.

"No, you don't see behind you." He smiled. "You're too busy looking ahead to notice around you."

"Is that a bad thing?"

"Not really, but you're a little like Nancy, people see you. People like you—"

"Well, that's a lie."

"It's not. You're guarded. I get it. You've seen the worst in people. You know what it means when people say one thing and don't mean it. This place isn't like anywhere else in the world, Meghan. You need to give it a chance."

She waited to speak. Calvin had her at a disadvantage. He'd done his homework on her. And unlike cursory looks at superficial internet searches,

Calvin was a journalist, and from what she'd read of his articles in the weekly *Northern Lights Sounder* he had a clear narrative that was objective without the need for self-promotion through slanted opinions that made journalistic articles more like sounding boards to influence readers.

"You know me apparently better than most."

"You need to get out more into the community. Let them see you as a person, not just a big coat with a badge on it."

"Hard to see a person that's constantly shivering all the time without that big coat."

It was a man's arctic weather coat. It was two sizes big on Meghan but long enough to dip below her knees. It kept her warm, that's what mattered.

"So, you didn't date Nancy?" she pressed.

Calvin shook his head. He collected the leftover Chinese-Mexican dishes. "Too much baggage for me," he said. "I live a minimal lifestyle. Nancy brought more than I ever wanted to carry around."

Satisfied with Calvin's answer, she collected her wits and stood up on tired legs. "I need to get back to work."

"Let me know if there's anything I can do."

Meghan gave him a look. She'd swept up her coppery waves into a disorganized mess on the back of her head. The hair was out of her eyes, and while she knew there were no beauty contests in town until July Fourth, Meghan was confident in her appearance. At least at a distance; she still needed a shower. "You've done a lot. Thank you, Calvin."

He smiled, a sweet smile on thin lips that made his hazel eyes sparkle under the fluorescent lighting. "You're welcome, Meghan."

Chapter Eleven

It wasn't until after midnight when Meghan locked up and left the office. She'd taken the time to plug in the block heater for the Suburban, so it fired up on the second try. Driving home in the dark, the rest of the town slept. Most everyone, that was, as Meghan considered, Brian and Cheryl were probably still awake. She knew Oliver was awake, or at least, awake enough to answer the text she sent him when she left the office.

Sometime yesterday, Nancy McCormick had company at her apartment, two people were alive and awake; afterward, one was dead. Meghan couldn't think straight and needed a few hours of sleep to clear the fuzzy junk in her head. She drove by the Snyder's house on her way home. There were lights on inside.

Shedding her clothes as she walked through the small one-bedroom house on Bison Street, Meghan made her way to the bathroom. One of the best features of the tiny house was the pressure and heat of the shower. It had new fixtures, and once she let it run hot, Meghan stepped under the steamy stream and tried scrubbing away the day.

The stippling puckered point where the bullet went into her body just above her right breast left a permanent reminder that life as a Special Agent for the FBI wasn't all about serving federal summons, or in-house casework. Outside the tundra of Alaska, wild churned and bubbled, melted slowly for the coming summer where the sun shown in the sky most of the day.

Villagers would be up late, out later, as the townspeople celebrated life anew. Someone took a slice of that life from Nancy McCormick, and Meghan wanted to know who in her tiny village miles from the real world wanted to disrupt harmony.

Meghan toweled off and wiped the steam from the mirror. The face she remembered looked back her. The body was a little chunkier than her day in the Bureau, but she wasn't running against the male-driven social status that bent the FBI around their social and formal strata. Meghan still turned heads. Not that she could see anyone while wearing a bulky hood. The coppery natural color and wavy hair drew attention. Unfortunately, hair conditioner was no match for the environment, and the wave lay limp against her hair a little longer than shoulder-length now. She had the obligatory green eyes that went with the recessive trait from a northern European lineage, a small rounded nose, and lips that were a little wide on her otherwise V-shaped face. When the sun caught her cheeks and across her nose, freckles sprang to life, it didn't often happen since moving to Alaska. She went up a size, maybe two, in her pants since moving to Kinguyakkii, and while Meghan meant to work off that added weight, it just wasn't part of her day anymore. Fast food was accessible to get; quicker to heat and eat, it was never meant to be kind to the hips.

She sighed, switched off the light, padded barefoot to the bedroom, and slipped into her sleepwear. Checking her phone for any texts from her on-duty officer, Meghan plugged the phone into the charger, set the alarm for four hours from now, and tried to sleep knowing there was still a killer out there and so far, he'd gotten away with it.

∗∗∗

Refreshed enough to focus, before she went to the office, Meghan drove by the trailer on Fifth Avenue and Lagoon Street, the porch light was on, and the rusty Ford Focus was there. While she didn't want to bother Calvin again, she needed something more and hoped he'd have the supplies.

After tapping lightly on the door, Meghan walked back to the truck. The ground chilled overnight enough to be crunchy underfoot.

"Everything okay?" Calvin asked from the doorway. He stood at the small steel stairs that led into the trailer. The *Northern Lights Sounder* placard by the door let everyone know it was a place of business.

Meghan faced him, swooped the hood off her head. "I thought you were working. I had another favor to ask."

He cocked an eyebrow smiling. "You'll owe me an exclusive when you catch the killer."

Meghan shook her head. "I don't think that's going to happen. We'll see that the troopers drop by, maybe, if they see fit to worry about it."

"Come inside. I got coffee on."

"Now, you're talking." She made her way up the corrugated steel stairs. Calvin retreated inside the trailer.

Meghan wiped her feet once inside and pulled shut the door. "I thought this was your office." She saw a small living room. The TV, a workstation with a large flat screen monitor, along with the kitchenette and the fresh aroma of coffee that permeated the warm air, down the small hallway she saw an unmade bed.

"It's my office. I work here. But I live here too." He took down two coffee mugs from the cupboard, poured measured coffee into each. From the refrigerator, he produced two flavored creamers. Meghan pointed to the vanilla. Once she had a cup in her hands, she took in the rest of the trailer. The workstation took up more space than the living room had to offer. There was a loveseat pushed against the kitchen counter. The corner desk took up the entire front of the area. Calvin was working on the latest edition of the weekly newspaper.

Meghan saw a photograph of Nancy McCormick on the front-page layout. It was a photo from the woman's social media files, not one of the pictures Meghan took at the crime scene.

"I'm going to write a biography of her. Something to let everyone know she was part of the community." He scrolled through the page layout for Meghan. She ignored the fact that Calvin crossed close to her on the way to the computer, his hand brushed against her shoulder. "Nothing about the murder," he added.

"I would think you'd write something about the murder."

He shook his head. "I don't have anything to write about right now. You haven't solved the crime," he said before sipping coffee. "People got enough to worry about here. We have problems with alcoholism, domestic violence. If you read the paper, you'd see I try to make things lighter, easier to digest."

"Still, people will talk about the murder."

"They will," he agreed with a nod. "People are already talking about it. My job, as far as I see it, is to tell the facts. Right now, all we have is a death. I want to write about justice."

"That's interesting coming from a reporter."

"I have readers North Slope Borough and Northwest Arctic Borough. I have subscribers from the lower-forty-eight for the online edition of the paper. I don't do this for the fame and certainly not the fortune. I don't make much money doing this. I teach too."

"You do?"

He nodded. "I have a master's in journalism; I'm an adjunct professor for the University of Alaska. They do tons of online courses. It helps pay the bills. Sometimes the school principal calls me when she needs someone to substitute for her. The paper is a hobby more than a career."

"This is nice." Meghan saw a framed newspaper article on the wall. It was a story about how the community of Kinguyakkii worked together to save a group of kids stranded on an ice flow that drifted out of the bay. Children had a habit of jumping on floating ice as a leisure pursuit, to combat boredom and challenge their friends. It was dangerous with ice chunks large enough to crush boat hulls in waters cold enough to cause hyperthermia in minutes. Kids only saw the adventures, not the trouble that went with it.

"That's the one, and the only time one of my articles was picked up by the *Associated Press*. It's a big deal for a journalist."

She needed to get back to work and addressed Calvin about why she woke him early that morning. "Did you have some photo printer paper? I've got the printer, and I want to get some pictures printed so I can take a look at the scene without straining my eyes on the computer."

Calvin went to a filing cabinet and opened the bottom drawer. He handed her a ream of paper.

"What do I owe you?"

"I'll send an invoice to the town."

"Duane will love that."

"Don't worry about him."

"Oh, I don't." She finished the coffee, put down the mug, and hoisted the package of paper in the air. "Thank you for this."

Meghan stepped out of the trailer. Calvin stood in the doorway in sweatpants and a t-shirt. It was as if the cold weather didn't bother him. "Are you going to sit down for that interview one of these days?"

"I might," she teased as she got into the Suburban.

Chapter Twelve

It was after eleven in the morning when Duane stormed into the police station. Meghan stood next to the table, staring at the rows of photographs she'd spent hours printing. She'd used almost the entire ream of paper Calvin gave her.

Duane was at the front where Lester sat at the counter, reading a magazine. "Hey!" he called when Meghan moved around the massive Formica table and into view from the archway separating the front counter from the rest of the business. Duane pushed through the small swinging café door that was supposed to keep the public from police business. "What happened to the supply of printer—" he stopped talking when he saw the dead eyes of Nancy McCormick staring at him from a few photographs on the tabletop. "What are you doing?"

"My job, Duane," Meghan said without looking up at him. "What do you want?"

"Shelley told me you took three months' worth of printer cartridges this morning."

"I needed color pictures, Duane. Hard to look at a crime scene in black and white," she said and put down another photo paper page, wet with laser ink. "You owe Calvin Everett for a ream of photo paper too."

"You can't do this. You can't do all of this." It was as if the crime scene photos were too much for Duane. Arms spread as he spoke as if presenting a buffet of murder on the table, his voice cracked and went up a few octaves. "You're not authorized to do this. You can't just make the rules around here. You're not going to solve this murder."

At that point, she'd heard enough. Meghan turned to Duane, narrowing her eyes. "What's that supposed to mean, Duane?" She moved around the far side of the table toward him. "Are you going to get in my way? Is there a reason you don't want me to solve this?" Five feet from him, Duane took a step backward. Lester watched the interaction by leaning over to look without having to get out of his chair.

There was no private place in the building to display the photographs. Meghan wanted to look at all the evidence, and the table was big enough for her to see it all. The welded seams of the conjoined contractor trailers leaked when it rained. Rusty trails had dripped down the walls, kept her from tacking the pictures to a wall. The roof over the table hadn't sprung a leak so far, and it was the best and only place to set out the scene.

"Why are you worried about me solving this, Duane?" Each step Meghan took forward, Duane took a step back. "Where were you on Saturday night? Do you have anyone who can vouch for your whereabouts?"

Duane's shoulder bumped into the archway as he backed away from Meghan. "You can't steal printer cartridges. We don't have enough money in the budget—"

"Screw your budget, Duane! A woman died here. Now I know that doesn't happen every day in your corner of the world. But where I come from, it happens a lot, and we'd like to go to bed at night and not have to worry about locking our doors because we have a killer walking around out there. Isn't that right, Officer Graves?"

"Sure enough, Chief." Lester used his foot to hold open the small swinging door for Duane. Once on the public side of the counter, the little door squeaked closed. Meghan stood beside Lester at the tall counter.

"Duane, you're not allowed back in here while we have an active investigation."

"You're supposed to call—"

"I called the State Troopers last night. I spoke to Detective Greg Anderson. I know you're going to run right next door after we have this chat and check on me. I don't care. Let me do my job, Duane. The town can afford a few more printer cartridges for the sake of this girl."

Duane said nothing when he left the office. The slamming door spoke loud enough.

"Lester, how about we lock the front door until this is all done."

"Sure thing, Chief," he answered, sliding off the chair long enough to pass through the little gate to lock the door.

Meghan went back to her table, studying the layout, looking at the pictures. She still had fingerprints to analyze but wanted to get a perspective of the scene. Lester timidly wandered through the archway to look at the pictures.

"Tell me what you see," Meghan said.

Lester took a moment to soak in the view. "I don't know. Looks a little disorganized."

Meghan looked up and smiled. "That's good. That's what I thought too."

"It was a man who killed her," he added confidently.

65

"I agree." She motioned to the bed, how the duvet looked. While Lester admitted to touching Nancy, checking for a pulse, he hadn't moved the blankets. "It looks like the killer threw the comforter over her in shame, in an afterthought."

"Was she..." he let the rest trail off.

Meghan shook her head. "Nancy wasn't sexually assaulted. She might have had consensual sex with the killer. But she wasn't raped before he strangled her." She took notes, reading the images, and writing down what she saw. "The killer robbed her, but only the money in the cookie tin — nothing like jewelry, not even the money in her wallet. I found credit cards and cash in the wallet. That tells me it was impulsive like something happened, and her death wasn't intentional."

"Any idea who did it?"

"Not yet. I think whoever killed Nancy is either still in town or one of the passengers on the flight out early Saturday morning. The troopers are following up with the list of people. I might have his fingerprints. I have to eliminate the known prints I have."

"That sounds like a lot of work." Lester moved back to the front counter. He settled in the chair. This time he put his boots on the shelf. With the front door locked, no one was going to notice him, even if he happened to doze a little.

"I'm going to head out for a while." She'd dressed in a knit cap and a coat that wasn't her oversized winter gear. Meghan put on gloves and wore her favorite pair of bunny boots. The boots were designed for arctic conditions with an extreme cold vapor barrier separating feet from the environment. The boots were expensive, but Meghan wanted to

keep her toes from frostbite. While it was only 38 F°
not cold enough to freeze toes, it was nice to have
warm feet when she spent so much time on them.
"Don't let anyone in that doesn't belong here.

"No problem, Chief."

Chapter Thirteen

The real estate company that managed Mountain Manor had a satellite office in Kinguyakkii. The sign on the door said someone would return to the office in fifteen minutes, but Meghan heard a male voice through the door. The first floor of the Chena Hotel on Shore Drive leased rooms for businesses. Sometimes people wanted to know what they were getting into before they built another building in town. The hotel catered to visitors who wanted to see what real Alaska was like, visit friends or family from Anchorage or the lower-forty-eight, or set up shop and test the cold waters.

Blue Sky Realty office was close to the fire exit. Meghan rapped on the door. The voice stopped talking. When no one came to the door, Meghan doubled-down on the knocking, this time with more authority.

The door opened to an unshaven face that looked around at Meghan from the edge of the door.

"I'm Chief Sheppard," she started. Her foot was already past the threshold where the door couldn't close. "Can I come in a minute?"

"Sure, sorry," he said. "I stepped out for lunch, forgot to take the sign off the door." He pulled the plastic clock off the nail on the outer door and tossed it to a nearby table. There was no bed in the room, only a desk, and a flat screen TV that showed a muted basketball game.

"I'm Nickolas Hodge. What can I do for you, Chief Sheppard?"

She shook hands with him before he sat down at the table. There was a shadow of Native Alaskan in him, the raven hair, and the athletic build. Rural Alaska was all about basketball, and either Hodge devoted a significant portion of the furnishings to division basketball teams with the overabundant sports paraphernalia or the real estate company invested in a team.

"I checked on a few things around town. I'm sure you heard what happened."

He nodded. Hodge sat down at his messy desk. He kept watching the television behind Meghan as she took a seat facing the desk.

"I'm curious if you've had any problems with tenants not making their rent."

He gave Meghan a look as if she'd presented him with a big shit sandwich and expected him to take a bite. "You're serious?"

"I am. Is there something wrong?"

"Well, it's just every time I want to get the police involved with tenants who don't pay their rent, my bosses tell me to leave it alone. They send these guys' certified letters, threaten to garnish wages and threaten eviction. But they never follow through."

"When you mean 'these guys' are you talking about anyone specifically?" she asked. Hodge had a bitter tone about his job, and it was her guess on whether or not that had to do with him living voluntarily or involuntarily in Kinguyakkii.

"I mean the tenants who don't pay rent."

"I take it there are a few."

Hodge laughed without humor. "Try about a third of the tenants in the building." He got up from the desk, went to a filing cabinet, and went through files. From various files, he pulled red copy paper. He made a stack of documents. Once collected, Hodge grabbed the papers and dropped them in front of Meghan on the desk. She made no move to look at them or pick up the papers. He pointed at the stack. "We got thirty units in that building. I've got about fifteen of those tenants who are behind on their rent. About five of those haven't paid rent all winter."

He dropped in the chair again, glanced to the score on the TV. "Now I get hounded by my bosses when these guys don't pay. They yell at me to take care of it. But they tie my hands. They tell me I got to do it civilly. That I can't call you to go and knock on their door, to get them to do something," he said, shoving the stack of papers on the desk. "My bosses come down on me, hold these telephone conferences from Seattle trying to help me get a handle on the morons who don't want to pay their rent."

Meghan cleared her throat. Hodge grabbed a pack of cigarettes from the coat hanging on the chair. Disregarding the 'no smoking' policy the hotel had, he lit a cigarette in front of the town cop with no regard for following the rules.

"I don't see how I'm supposed to collect money from them when my company isn't willing to file charges against the tenants."

"Is there anyone who was recently behind and suddenly made a payment, between Saturday and today?"

"Yeah, sure," he mumbled, pressing the cigarette between his lips, Hodge dug through the various stacks of paper on his desk, if there was a filing system Meghan didn't see it. Hodge found what he wanted and handed it to Meghan. "This guy lives on the third floor of the apartment building. He paid two months back rent on Monday morning. He paid in cash."

Meghan suppressed, raising her eyebrows when the buzzer went off in her head. "What about Nancy McCormick?" she asked. "She ever fall behind on her rent?"

"I don't know, maybe. I'd have to look. I know she was never thirty-days or sixty-days past due. I got one family that's one hundred fifty days past due. Can you do anything about them?"

"The real estate company has to go through the legal channels, take the tenant to small claims court. You know how it is here, you can't just evict someone when its winter in Alaska."

"Yeah, I know—I know, but it's always winter in Kinguyakkii. Nothing like a little bad press toward the real estate company," he added. Hodge snuffed out the cigarette in the overflowing ashtray on the desk. He immediately lit a second cigarette. "I even went and talked to the mayor of this town. He was no help at all."

"You're not from around here, are you?"

"Hell no," he said venomously. "I'm from Palmer. This kind of thing happened in Palmer and the police would throw out people into the streets. I can't wait to get out of here." The last part came out as if a verbalized thought and wasn't meant for Meghan. She chose to ignore it.

Meghan said nothing about Hodge's smoking, choking her air supply or his attitude toward locals. She didn't know if the rules were different in Palmer than Kinguyakkii, but the court wasn't interested in people freezing to death in the bush.

71

Hodge pointed the glowing end of the cigarette at Meghan. "Any chance of me getting Nancy's apartment rented? I got people on the waiting lists that have a clear background and credit checks if I can get into her apartment that would be great."

Meghan stood up. She needed fresh air since it dissipated in the office. Hodge watched the game a little more. "Tell you what I can do. First, we're in the middle of an active police investigation, so the apartment isn't available any time soon. But why don't you print off a list of tenants who are behind on their rent? Include the tenant who made the back rent recently."

Hodge stood, scooped the red copy papers he'd pulled initially from the tenant files and tried to hand them to Meghan. She shook her head.

"I'd like fresh copies."

"It'll take time, and I gotta print them off." There was a hint of annoyance in his voice as if he wanted the police to help but wasn't willing to put in the effort to accommodate her.

"That's fine. I'll wait." She moved away from the front of the desk and looked at the rest of the office. The basketball jerseys on the wall, the bookshelf had trophies and other memorabilia. "You play?"

"I did in college. I screwed up my knee. Lost my scholarship," Nickolas spoke as he worked on the laptop. The printer whirred to life began spitting fresh late notices.

"You went to college in Alaska?"

"I started in Alaska. My second term I transferred to Seattle. I ended up in Arizona after I hurt my knee. I got my real estate license there, but you know how hard it is to sell a house?"

"No idea." She'd made her way along the available wall, looking at high school pictures, trophies with Nickolas Hodge's name on the placards.

"Nancy came back from Arizona three years ago."

"I was living in Phoenix. I think Nancy was from Mesa. I saw that on her application." He smiled and added, "feels like a small world sometimes. You travel three thousand miles and run into someone from your home state.

"You ran into her in Arizona. You ever get to know her?" There was abuzz in her head — crosses between talking to people that were suspects, and the general public. Aged law enforcement officers, LEOs eventually spoke to everyone the same, the defaulted to the negative side of interviews. It wasn't that older cops thought everyone was suspect; they merely realized that everyone was suspicious of something; it was the level of the crime that mattered after a while.

"No, see her around sometimes. See her here a lot. You know, small town. See her at least once a month when she dropped off rent." The late noticed printed out. Hodge gathered them, tamped the edges of the paper on the desk and handed them to Meghan. "You get the guy who killed her yet?"

This time she couldn't stop her eyebrows from darting upward. "The guy?" she asked.

"Well, yeah. I mean come on, a hot chick like Nancy must have been a guy that killed her."

"Okay." She lifted the papers. "Did you include the guy who paid yesterday?"

73

"Yeah, his late noticed was still from last month. Can you get these people to pay? I would appreciate that."

"I'll see what I can do."

Hodge finished the second cigarette. He snubbed out the smoldering tip in the ashtray and went around the desk as Meghan went for the door. He had that look in his eye that told Meghan what to expect next. Nickolas Hodge was the type-A personality kind of guy who, as Cheryl suggested of Nancy, 'peaked in high school.' He was handsome in a compelling way, a former ballplayer, tall enough to have to look up when he was still a few feet away from her. He was a few years younger than Meghan, around Nancy's age. "So, you married, Chief?"

Once upon a time, it was rumored Alaska's ratio of men to women was a hundred to one. Closer figures put the ratio at five to one; but a guy like Hodge, a man who wasn't afraid to complain about tenants, make inflammatory statements about tenants in a racial context, he'd hit on anyone, like a freshwater eel in Alaska; they were always around, you just didn't want to hook one.

It took everything she had to hold back, laughing out loud. He was too confident, too sure of himself. Here she was in the middle of a murder investigation, Hodge wanted to investigate Meghan's bedroom.

"I'm in a relationship," she said lightly. It was true if that relationship had to do with her career. She opened the door and stepped into the hallway, retreating from the layer of blue cigarette smoke. "Thanks for the notices. I'll be in touch."

Hodge took the message as an encouraging sign. Reaching into the pocket of his slacks, he removed a silver case and opened it. The business card was expensive. The kind A-list realtors used to impress their clients. "My cell phone is on there. Give me a call."

"Thank you," she said, collecting the card and heading toward the lobby. She didn't have to look back to know Hodge was watching her ass as she walked away.

Meghan got into the Suburban, dropped the stack of papers on the passenger seat, tossed the business card in the center column, and started the car. She pressed her sleeve to her nose, and then pulled at her hair, pressed it to her nose. The clothes and her clean hair both smelled like cigarettes.

Chapter Fourteen

There was no such thing as garden variety controversy with Duane. While gardens weren't hard to maintain in Alaska, they grew very well during the summer months, most often below the polar circle, Duane usually planted negativity and allowed it to flourish. If it wasn't receipts and invoices for printer cartridges and photo paper, there was something else planted and bubbled to the surface. Granted, Meghan knew before it happened that he'd fume over the latest surprise.

"You know there's no smoking in company vehicles." It was as if the announcement had merit. She knew the mayor smoked, even smoked in his pickup truck. That truck had a town decal on the doors. Somehow, hypocrisy was biased.

She'd once found an apple wedged under the rear seat of the Suburban. It was ancient and shriveled. Not only did it look a little like Mother Theresa it miraculously managed to sprout a shoot from the area that sunlight scratched through the window and shone against the back seat. Obliged to do something noble after feeling guilty about removing it from the balanced interior, Meghan buried it in the ground.

Kinguyakkii once had a designated forest of one tree, a cultivated dogwood that needed tending and care because the environment was too inhospitable for it to grow without nurturing. A few years before Meghan arrived, a disgruntled employee of the North Slope Borough Council cut it down with a hatchet in a final fit of frustration against the Council Members who wouldn't vote in favor of planting more trees and allocating funds for someone to maintain the single tree forest.

When she faced Duane towering over her, peering at her as if still trying desperately to intimidate her or possibly set her on fire with an evil look, he had an agenda that went well beyond her, Meghan knew that.

His brother-in-law wanted to be the Chief of Police. Only Meghan ran without competing and had a zero-end game without trying. North Slope Borough Council members hired her because she had applied for the job, mostly. The fact that she has a bachelor's degree in criminal justice, a Master's in Sociology, and a minor in Public Safety Administration put her as top and only candidate for the position. The fact she was a retired Special Agent for the FBI was just gravy. Duane's brother had criminal associates in Seattle, worked as an attorney in a less than a reputable law firm, had something to do with less intellectually challenged members of the Council to pass on him, in favor of Meghan.

"I don't smoke, Duane." She breezed through the gateway separating police from civilians. Lester stood like a lonely tree in a forgotten forest in front of the small door and hadn't let Duane pass. "What do you want? I'm busy."

"I got a receipt for a special-order package, an Express Mail from Quantico, Virginia."

Meghan shrugged out of her jacket, turned to Duane still hovering on the civilian side of the counter. "Where's my package?" she demanded.

Duane made a face that was caught between annoyed and irritable bowel. "We don't get Express Mail in Kinguyakkii, do you know why?" It was rhetorical, and Meghan sighed because she knew he'd— "Because the United State Post Office sends a special carrier out with the package. You know we have to pay for the fuel charges."

"Oh please, we live in the United States, Duane, it can't be that—oh, right." He presented the cost of shipping the package. The bill was almost as much as the order. "Well, okay. But we needed it."

"You're not getting it." It was a finality that wasn't open for debate. Duane turned and left the office. The exit door hung open for a while after he stepped down to the gravel and started marching across space between the police station and Town Hall. The wind caught the door and slammed it. Lester gave Meghan a look of satisfaction and sat down again.

Too heated up to grab the jacket, Meghan went through the little gateway and out the door. She closed it behind her instead of letting it slam. The chilly northern breeze pushed at her hair, coated her face and hands, the exposed skin with icy fingers. Meghan hurried to Town Hall.

She went through the front door. Unlike the police station, leftover contractor trailers, Kinguyakkii Town Hall was a real business. Built with aesthetic charm, the aluminum roof kept snow from building up, the ivory façade was just enough of color to pick out the building within snowdrifts during the winter. Inside was a plush waiting room with leather sofas, a walnut coffee table, and current subscriptions to hunting and fishing magazines. Town Hall never received enough visitors for anyone other than Duane to read the magazines.

Shelley Bass was Duane's office administrator. She looked up from the face of her smartphone, and the pleasant smile evaporated as soon as she saw

Meghan glaring at her. "Mr. Warren is leaving for the evening, Meghan. He said not to disturb him."

Meghan looked beyond the perfect raven hair, the salon nails, and expensive eye shadow. Shelley would be pretty if she didn't have such a miserable demeanor. She was perfect for Duane.

Meghan was about to storm back to Duane's office down the small corridor with soft LED lighting and commissioned Alaskan landscape paintings on the walls. Then she saw what she wanted, why she'd followed Duane across the property.

"You can't touch that." Shelley swiveled in the high-back black leather chair at her cherry wood desk. She didn't get up.

Meghan grabbed the Express Mailbox. She saw the handwriting on the receipt. Carrying it back to Shelley's desk, Meghan kept her temper.

"You should know, Shelley, that I am, like it or not, the Chief of Police. Now I know you work for Duane, but I work for the North Slope Borough Council, and while technically Duane is my boss, only in the very loosest sense of the word, I am not governed by him. Or you." Meghan made sure she tilted the package, so the paperwork affixed to the top showed at Shelley. "Did you know it's a federal offense to sign another person's name to a piece of mail? You misspelled my name. It's already here, you didn't refuse the package, and since you signed for it, it now belongs to me." She gave Shelley her best smile. "Thank you."

Carrying the package out into the weather, Meghan didn't bother closing the door behind her, letting the wind push at the door until Shelley had to leave the safety of the desk to close and lock it.

79

Chapter Fifteen

The Ammattauq Native Trader Store was a little less traditional now than it probably was a hundred years ago. There were two stores in Kinguyakkii. Meghan did her shopping at a typical grocery and general merchandise store. There was an art to ordering fresh fruit, meats, and dairy in rural Alaska and expecting the product to arrive before the shelf life terminated or the meat spoiled. So far, she'd been lucky, and the store managers at the franchise market were savvy about maintaining customers by keeping fresh food stocked on the shelves. Even in Kinguyakkii, it was impossible to compete with online ordering. It took a little longer to get orders, but the post office was usually busier than any other business in town.

Eric Kennedy managed the store. He had a knack for remembering everyone he saw by name. He was a lifelong Alaskan and had a lot of respect for the traditional values that were lost on most everyone else in the southern states; and in Alaska, they were all southern states.

"What can I do for you tonight, Chief Sheppard?" He wore a blue apron while he stocked the shelves. His paunch stuck out like he was a pregnant man about to be famous for an impossible condition. The shop was filled with mostly camping equipment, fishing supplies, and non-perishable foods in cans. He sold condensed milk by the case because some people liked to drink it like a can of soda. The stack of three-gallon tubs of vegetable shortening was an essential ingredient for some classic tundra recipes. Sugar was sold in ten pound and twenty-five pound bags, not meager five pound bags. When people were snowed in for a month, it was good to have food supplies that kept up the calories when they had to wait a few weeks to dig out of the drifts or get back to town.

The trader store was an extension of the Native Alaskan cultural and hosted by the North Slope Borough. Trappers brought animal hides, sides of caribou, seal oil, seal and whale steaks. They traded the items over the counter with Eric as a mediator to make sure everyone received their fair market share. It wasn't a job for the squeamish and certainly something Meghan could do because it was challenging to think about the environment when Native Alaskans wanted to continue to live off the land. They had every right, and she respected it. Eric made sure the product was safe, and the North Slope Borough kept detailed records for fish and game state regulators.

"I wanted to check on Nancy."

Eric wiped his hands. He'd been filleting halibut steaks. He put the knife in the sink behind the glass cooler counter and washed his hands. While he dried them on the apron, he motioned for Meghan to follow him through the backroom doors.

The walk-in freezer wasn't part of the original building. It was once a trailer for a refrigeration truck. When the additions for the trading store happened, they added onto the store by building around the cooler trailer. It ran off town electric, but if the power went out, it had backup generators.

She tried ignoring the stacks of muktuk on the shelves, hard to get more traditional Alaskan than frozen whale skin and blubber.

"She's safe and sound." Eric stood back, allowing Meghan to give the body a quick look. They had wrapped her in the sheets from the bed with

81

bungee straps not too tight around the body to keep the sheets against her and secure her legs and arms for transport. Meghan put on medical gloves before she did anything else.

She rolled back the sheet away from Nancy's face and neck. She got closer. There was purplish bruising that showed up more around Nancy's throat.

"What's that?" he asked, looking at the kit Meghan brought with her, "Looks expensive."

"It is." Meghan squatted next to the steel table in the cooler and opened the FBI latent fingerprint kit she'd ordered and had express shipped to her from Quantico. The other prints Meghan took at the apartment were good; she didn't need to print them again. But she wanted the genuine kit to use to attempt fingerprints from Nancy's face and neck.

Eric stood by, quietly watching Meghan work. She was delicate and deliberate with dusting and collecting. When she got what she wanted from Nancy, Meghan put away the collection equipment.

"Do you have a tissue or paper towel?" she asked.

Eric grabbed a clean dish towel and handed it to Meghan. He watched her wipe off the excess powder from the body. "Do you know what Cheryl and Brian are planning for her?" he asked.

"I don't know. I haven't talked to them about it. I wanted to get Nancy to Anchorage for an autopsy. The report I sent to the state troopers seemed to satisfy them enough with my preliminary report. They're in no hurry to open her up."

"Yeah," Eric said. "This isn't the sort of thing that happens around here."

"She wasn't assaulted, and I don't know if I collected anything usable from her." Meghan touched Nancy's hair, brushed it into place.

"Her hyoid bone's crushed," Eric mentioned indifferently.

"How can you tell?" She looked at Nancy again.

"Oh, before I brought her to the cooler, I went by the clinic and had her X-rayed for you."

Meghan shook her head. She followed Eric out of the cooler and further into the back storeroom. It was tidy and stocked full. He had a friendly office with a collection of equipment that balanced between the store manager and coroner. There was an X-ray light board on the back wall. He found the X-ray slides and put up two of Nancy's neck. "See here," he said, pointing to the neck.

The U-shaped bone in the upper neck was meant to support the human tongue. The hyoid bone was delicate and didn't take a lot of pressure to crush. The X-ray showed Nancy's hyoid was more M-shaped than U-shaped. "It tore into the thyroid cartilage here," he said pointing. "Rarely occurs in fractures, most of the time it breaks during strangulation. What?"

Meghan was smiling at him. "I am impressed, Eric. You went above and beyond. I didn't even think to get Nancy X-rayed."

"I do what I can, Chief." He puffed up at the compliment. "I know Brian and Cheryl don't have a lot of money to have her sent to Anchorage for cremation."

"What do you think they'll want to do?"

"Well, usually the town gets together, and we'll dig her grave out there in the cemetery. Kinguyakkii Cemetery was a hodge-podge planting of loved ones in the village. Some people afforded the shipping charges for cremation. Others had to wait for spring and summer to break ground and dig deep enough to put their loved ones in the ground. There was one granite headstone in the cemetery; someone had it shipped from Anchorage in the 1970s. Most of the time, people whittled crosses out of saplings from downriver or carved their one designed headstone from rocks found along the shoreline or somewhere on the tundra. "It won't be until June or July before the ground's thawed enough for us to bury Nancy."

"Can you keep her that long in here?" she asked delicately. There had to be some regulations about storing food products near corpses. It wasn't Meghan's jurisdiction, and she had enough on her plate to worry about.

"I'll do what I can for the family."

"Did you know her?"

"Everyone knew Nancy. I never dated her." He held up his left hand, flashing his ring finger.

"You're married. I didn't know that."

"Well, you don't come in here. She's around sometimes. My wife helps me with some of the village elders who don't want to speak English. We know they're coming to town with something special, like carved ivory, jade jewelry, or gold, Linda comes in to greet them. I want to make sure they get a fair trade for their stuff. And I contact the Alaska Native Heritage Center if any of the crafts are antique. I can't trade most of the stuff that's too old, but I can put the family in touch with curators."

"You deal in antiquities?" Meghan glanced around the backroom. It was a typical storeroom. Near the back, close to the rear exit, there was a modern cage that went from floor to ceiling. At the question, Eric motioned for Meghan to take the added step to see inside the locked cage.

There were hand carved ivory pieces from walrus harvest, bone carvings, chunks of metal and rock — a collection of Alaska artisan masks, skin drums, figurines covered in fur kuspuks. The shelves were filled with a native museum's dream collection.

"I hold onto a lot of these for elders. Sometimes the young generations think it's just something to pass along, make a little money for trade. If I get something from one of the older families, something that I think has been handed down, I'll make a deal, get Linda involved, and we have a guy that flies out from Anchorage to date the artifacts. If they think it's something important, Linda gets involved, and we start real negotiations. She speaks Inupiaq, Yup'ik, and a little Athabaskan." He smiled and shrugged proudly.

"That's good to know in case I run into any language barriers." Meghan thumbed at the large lumps of dirty rocks on the bottom plates of the metal shelves inside the cage. "Are those what I think they are?"

Eric saw the hunks of dirty rocks with small breaks in the mud that caught the light and flashed goldenly. "Yeah," he said with a modest nod. "I get those sometimes. When I do, I set up an account with the owner. They usually get whatever they want in trade, and the gold is like a credit account. Sometimes I have to cash-in one of those." They walked away from the cage. Meghan glanced at the very simple padlock on the steel cage. She had enough on her plate to worry about the dollar value in the Alaskan art or the few pounds of gold casually lying on the floor in a small trading post store.

"Most of the time the elders don't speak English because they don't want to, you know that." He was more than met the eye, Meghan suddenly realized. She felt ashamed in thinking people living in rural Alaska were straightforward, narrow-minded people. She realized while they were unfussy, many of her neighbors made decisions to live in an inhospitable environment out of choice, not a necessity. "Linda can strike up a conversation with anyone. She's great at bartering too. The university uses her language skills sometimes when they need correct pronunciations."

"Like when people mispronounce Kinguyakkii."

He smiled. "Just like that, you're close, but not too many people get it right."

"I'll work on it. Thank you for your help, Eric." She'd underestimated him. Aside from the unorthodox approach to handling the dead, Eric turned out to be an asset instead of a liability.

Chapter Sixteen

The name at the top of her list was a neighbor down the hall from Nancy McCormick. According to the late notice list Nickolas printed for Meghan from the Blue Sky Realty tenants, Vincent Atkinson caught up three months back rent in a day. That was a lot of cash all at once. While Cheryl wasn't confident about the amount of money in the cookie tin, she knew Nancy was frivolous, more than she could afford. There were a lot of online ordered shoes in the dead woman's closest. The type of shoes no one in Kinguyakkii could wear, except maybe on a Thursday afternoon in mid-August when they got a warm, sunny day.

Cheryl suspected there might have been between a thousand to fifteen hundred in cash. While that wasn't enough to pay three months back rent, it was a chunk of money that was stolen during the murder. Meghan was almost sure; money wasn't the motivating factor for Nancy's death. The woman was impulsive. Meghan sat in the driver's seat of the Chevy staring up at the face of the Mountain Manor apartment complex. Most of the windows had drawn shades, some had cardboard over the windows or aluminum foil, trapping heat in and midnight sun out when the sun happened. It was like Christmas decorations in March. Some people just left them up because Christmas came back around again, eventually.

There were too many people in the complex to question about Nancy's murder. Meghan knew that immediately. That's why she wanted to focus on what was inside the apartment, not around it. The money was one way to narrow the search parameters.

"Hey Boss," Oliver said when he rolled up to Mountain Manor where Meghan had parked. The building had several stanchions that protected the place from larger vehicles, while snowmobiles and four-wheelers got closer to the building. Oliver pulled up and parked the Polaris close to the Suburban. "What did you need?"

Meghan wanted backup when she questioned the suspect. Since it was after eight on Tuesday night, and ice fog rolled across the tundra from the bordering tundra fields, pushing into the bay. Kinguyakkii was nestled on a gravel spit of a peninsula that reached into Kinguyakkii Bay. It was a perfect launch point for barges and vessels under a hundred and twenty feet designed for shallow water. The bay wasn't deep enough for luxury boats, which meant unlike Juneau and Ketchikan, Alaska, tourists had to take flights into the town or crawl along the shoreline. Outside the low protective mountains that protected the harbor, the chop of the Bering Sea wasn't the ideal water fun people expected when they boarded cruise ships.

"How well do you know Vincent Atkinson?" she asked, reading his name from the list Hodge gave her.

Oliver scratched his chin after removing the heavy gloves he used riding the four-wheeler. "His family lives in Kivalina. He's working at the store there, as far as I know." Lester went home for the evening, Oliver had the night shift, and Meghan had a few hours off here and there when there wasn't something pressing, she had to solve, like a murder.

"Well, I want to have face to face with him, and I wanted you as a backup." They started walking together into the apartment complex. Through the foyer, tenants moved to the side for her and Oliver, nodding in recognition. Other than the oversized winter coat, the rusty blue Suburban, and the Kinguyakkii police patch on her jacket, Meghan was just another sexless person wearing cold weather gear at the tail-end of March when anywhere else in the US snows departed and new life sprang from spring grounds.

"Looks like ice fog coming," Oliver commented about the layer of white mist that tinkled when it hit metal as it drifted through town. "Could last a couple of days," he added. He knew his weather, knew the people in town, and with a body like a solid brick of ice, Meghan was glad to have Oliver around when it came to moving people who didn't want to be touched or move on their own.

They made their way upstairs through the stairwell that was closest to Nancy's apartment. On the third floor, Apartment 3E was taped off with yellow caution tape and duct tape. It wasn't pretty, but it kept people out of the crime scene.

Heavy boots plodded down the hall to Apartment 3G where Meghan knocked on the door. She unzipped the outerwear because the hallway was pushing 80°F.

The television inside the apartment was loud enough to hear the canned laughter from a rerun of a sitcom. The door opened, a short Inuit man with black socks, prescription glasses, and a round belly stood before Meghan and Oliver. She felt better about having to take him down if he made a run for it. She was eye to eye with him.

"Vincent Atkinson?" she asked, ready to start questioning him.

"Hey, Vince," Oliver said. "We're here because Nancy's dead and we want to know if you killed her."

Meghan felt the breath catch in her throat. While she wanted Oliver to join her for safety sake, and it was good for him to shadow her when she interrogated suspects, he made a preemptive accusation that could have gone awry quickly.

Instead of running, or maybe shooting both of the police officers, Vincent sniggered. "Eh, what?"

"Is it okay if we come in?" she asked. It took no time at all to draw a crowd. Already neighbors were poking out their heads, watching Oliver and Meghan harass one of the neighbors in the building.

Oliver moved into the apartment ahead of Meghan. She made eye contact with the older adult across the hall from Vincent before closing the door behind her. It was a look of 'you're next' that hopefully got through to him to close the door and stay out of the way.

Inside the apartment, Vincent went back to the small love seat and dropped on worn out cushions that formed to his large rump. There was a bag of cheese puffs in front of him on the coffee table and a two-liter bottle of soda without a glass. Vincent was catching up on binge-watching cable comedy shows and on his way to early diabetes. He switched off the television.

"So, I'm following up on your neighbor."

"Yeah, Nancy," he said.

"Well, I'm curious about how you managed to pay three months back rent on Monday."

A cheese puff paused just outside the mouth agape as Vincent looked from Meghan to Oliver and back again. Inserting the puff, he talked around it. "What's that got to do with Nancy dying?"

"Well, there—ow." Oliver rubbed his arm where Meghan poked him with her pen from taking notes. She glared at him to keep quiet before addressing Vincent.

"I got a letter from Blue Sky Realty; they own this building. It says here you were three months behind on your rent until yesterday. I'm curious where all the money came from."

Vincent didn't look insulted; he sighed and shook his head. He stared at the blank screen of the TV. "I had to borrow some money from my gram. I ain't proud of it. I don't get enough hours at the store, you know?"

Meghan took in the rest of his apartment. He didn't have high standards when it came to clothing or furniture. Even his boots were older. Meghan was reasonably satisfied that even a conscientious murderer wouldn't use stolen money to pay back rent on an apartment a few doors down from the girl who was murdered. It was a lost cause. She knew the moment Vincent opened the door. Nonetheless, the due process sometimes took a few loose turns before it turned right again.

✳✳✳

Back outside, Oliver straddled the Polaris after running a glove over the seat to clear the moisture. Meghan needed to get back to the station. Oliver was officially on duty, but over the last few days, between him and Lester, they had logged a lot of hours, and one thing the town never did was pay overtime.

"Can you field any calls tonight from your house?" she asked. "I'm heading back to the department to do some work. I'll probably be working late again. If you don't get any calls, stay home. If something comes up, I'll give you a call. That okay?"

"Sure, Boss." He grinned and started the Polaris. "Hey, I got a call yesterday from a pilot says someone was siphoning fuel out of his plane again."

Meghan nodded. "When are the next snowmachine races?" While the rest of the world called snowmobiles—well, snowmobiles, real Alaskans called them snowmachines. It was essential to fit in whenever possible, and while it didn't seem like much, villagers respected when people called them by their proper names.

"Not for a while, eh?" Winter was officially over. There was still snow lingering in places, and the races were significant when the lakes and rivers were solid ice and opened for racings. People used airplane fuel in their snowmachines because it burned hotter and faster than regular gas. He laughed and swung the four-wheeler around in a U and accelerated out to Wolverine Drive where the oncoming Durango slammed on brakes and blasted a horn. "Sorry," Oliver shouted, waving to the driver.

Meghan climbed into the Suburban shaking her head. If her officer was trying for a cool exit, he'd failed miserably. She still needed to address the conversation he started with Vincent, abruptly accusing him of murder as soon as he opened the door. Oliver was a good cop, just needed a little refining.

Chapter Seventeen

Meghan switched on the local AM radio station. It was a non-profit station that started broadcasting in 1975. With state and federal grants, the radio station had a range that reached, depending on the weather, all the way to the zinc mines. Even with the limited range, people used it to communicate upcoming bingo events, birthday wishes, and potluck dinners at the church. Once in a while, people sent oral messages to other villages, calling into the station to have the communiqué transmitted a few hundred miles because cell phones didn't reach outside the city; impossible to use a cell phone without a cell tower nearby.

That night Meghan had the radio on for background noise and to see if there was any broadcast news of Nancy McCormick's death. Since the local newspaper intended to run a biography on the woman, thanks to Calvin, there wasn't any competing news coverage that updated the fact there was still a killer loose.

The smartphone buzzed on the table next to Meghan while she was concentrating, startling her as she read the text. Smiling, she stood up. Veering toward the bathroom to check her hair, straighten the sweatshirt, pulling it down on her hips, Meghan went to the front door and unlocked it.

"You know, people are going to talk if you keep coming here," she said.

Calvin chortled as he carried a pizza box through the door. There was a bag on the lid and by the smell of it, garlic sticks inside the container.

"What are you working on tonight?" he asked, seeing the table was covered in the collection of makeshift fingerprints.

Meghan collected and stored the evidence photographs in her office. The fingerprints were going to yield better results, as far as she could tell. Eating was something that she'd forgotten since the murder. It wasn't healthy to go without food, forgetting to eat, but Calvin wasn't helping when he brought an extra-large pizza and expected her to eat it with him. She had to draw the line.

"I don't think it's a good idea you keep coming here, bringing me food." She talked as Calvin went to the small counter where the coffee pot sat, still warm and now empty. He grabbed a paper plate, dropped a slice of pizza on the plate, then used a napkin to pick up a breadstick and put it on top of the pizza. He shoved it at Meghan.

"You eat; I'll leave if you want." He added the last part after a pause that was meant to elicit some guilt from her for bringing more food. He looked at the laptops with the scanner and the collection of fingerprint cards made with packing tape. He lifted one to look at it and brought it closer to his nose to smell it. "This smells like burnt matches."

"I had to improvise." She carried the plate back to the main table where she'd been working. It was already on the plate; she had to eat at least that slice; and the garlic breadstick.

Calvin placed the card on a stack of similar cards. He looked at the program on the screen of the laptop.

"You're checking fingerprints in the national database?" He sat down in the available chair beside Meghan.

She had to finish chewing, covering her mouth with a napkin before answering him. "I don't have

94

access to the database. That costs a lot of money. I did download the program to scan and analyze the fingerprint based on known and unknown prints."

Calvin slapped his hands together and rubbed. "What can I do to help?" There were two laptops; she downloaded the program on both computers, one for the department and one on her personal laptop for the backup.

"Officially, there's nothing you can do." The pizza tasted great. For some reason, even with the scent of garlic on the breadstick, Meghan could still smell Calvin's refreshing aftershave. It wasn't just sleep and food that Meghan had denied herself when she took the job as chief of police.

"Are you going to say something like I'm a suspect and I'm inserting myself into the investigation because that's what crazy people do?"

"Well, maybe not that, as far as I know." There was a little tiny red flag that went up in Meghan, but it was too hard to see past the hazel eyes.

"Then let me help. I have great attention for detail, and this looks like something that needs attention. You've got two programs here. Did you scan all the fingerprints? I can do that."

"They're all scanned."

"Then let me categorize them for you. I see you've used a numbering system. You made a map of the apartment. I can make sure they're matched to the rooms of the apartment."

"For someone who is supposed to be a casual observer, you sure are making yourself an obvious suspect."

"If you want me to insert myself, I can do that too." The smile faded. She saw the look change because something in Calvin, the right person that understood someone was dead and this wasn't a game, that person knew how important it was that she did everything in her power to see the person who killed Nancy was brought to justice.

"I know this is important," he started. "I know it feels like you're against the entire world. You care what happened."

"It gets me in trouble."

"How can doing your job get you in trouble?"

"I know, right? But tomorrow morning, the mayor is going to come storming into this office and want to know why I spent town money on a software program for fingerprints."

"Can't be that expensive," Calvin said offhandedly. The look on her face suggested that he was wrong. "Well, if you get something from all this then it was worth the price you paid for it."

Meghan sat back in the chair. One slice of pizza wasn't filling that hole in her gut, but she wasn't about to go for a second slice with Calvin sitting right beside her. She finished off the breadstick.

"I feel like no one wants me to do my job." Meghan stood, put away the paper plate, wiped her face, and went into the small bathroom to wash her hands. "The detective from Anchorage is indifferent about all this. I talked to him again a few hours ago, and he told me they were doing everything on their end. I don't even know what that means." She stood watching Calvin, turned around to look at her from the chair. He was handsome and trying to be helpful, and

Meghan knew she only needed one of those at the moment.

"Let me show you what I'm doing," she started and retook the seat beside him. The radio station played a mono version of a classic pop song from the 1960s. It wasn't the kind of music anyone wanted for a montage. Over the next hour, they worked quietly side by side, processing the fingerprints that Meghan collected throughout the apartment.

There were three prints she focused on after eliminating Nancy, Cheryl, and Brian's fingerprints from the crime scene.

"So, you've got this print here you wanted me to check the others against." Calvin sat back, pushing away from the table, rubbing his eyes. "This print matches the one in the bedroom."

Meghan felt a flash of excitement. She looked at the two prints on the screen. The computer software program put them as matches. There were two different prints from two separate locations. Both match up to the one in the bedroom.

"Which one are you comparing it to?" Meghan leaned over to look at the laptop screen. She pressed her shoulder against Calvin. She tried to ignore him as she looked at the numbers of the prints.

Grabbing the note, she used to mark the print locations, Meghan frowned. While she wanted to relay the information to Calvin, Meghan stopped before any words left her mouth. The numbering system didn't have any names on the list. She omitted names because she wanted to use only a number system to eliminate any chances of bias reporting.

The individual scan came from the nightstand. She'd lifted it clean of the other overlapping fingerprints of Nancy's impressions. The labeling system she used had the prints belonging to suspect #2.

"Is this the killer?" Calvin asked of the 99.3% accuracy of the compared data. The whorls, ridges, and double loops were identical to ones she'd collected from individuals known to Nancy.

"I—I can't tell you that," she said. Her words seem to hurt Calvin. He stood up, moving away from her. She was honest. It wasn't that it had nothing to do with him. He wasn't even part of the police department. In some circles, the reporter was the antagonist in the story. Calvin was a misplaced hero, at best. She wanted to explain it wasn't that she didn't want to tell him, it was a simple fact; Meghan wasn't sure if the print found on the nightstand belonged to the killer or if it was something else.

"I need to get going." He slipped on his coat, gloves, and ski cap. Before he departed, leaving the leftover pizza and breadsticks, he gave Meghan and heartfelt look. "I know you're just doing your job. I have no right to get in the way, but I'd be lying if I wasn't worried for you."

"Thank you, Calvin. Really, I appreciate what you've done."

"Yeah, no problem," he said, moving through the small swinging gate, unlocking the door. "I'll see you later." When Calvin opened the door, warm air from inside the police station slammed against the wall of ice fog that built up outside. The fog rolled into the waiting area before Calvin slammed the door behind him.

Meghan went back to the computer. She pulled up the list of suspects. It wasn't necessary. She used her prints in the system, along with Lester's, Oliver's, Nancy's, Brian's and Cheryl's prints as part of the control group. Each of them, including her, was assigned 'suspect' and a number. Out of the control group, one of the fingerprints was in a place it shouldn't be, a member of the control group wasn't telling the truth about their association with Nancy.

Chapter Eighteen

The thing about death, whether natural or not, it got in the way, but life went on afterward. Cheryl and Brian had a business to run. They were down a waitress, and people in town deposited money in a tip jar with Nancy's name on it out of respect. They had to keep working, taking even a few days off put them behind on everything and while they didn't have competition, people in town still had expectations.

"What did you find out?" Cheryl asked when she saw Meghan walk through the front door of the café on Wednesday morning.

The place was full of people, and no one breathed or spoke upon realizing that the chief of police walked through the front door and was immediately called out by the victim's sister.

"Is there somewhere we can talk?" she asked quietly. Standing at the cashier counter, watching Brian and Cheryl's expectant faces wasn't helping the situation.

"Come on out back," Brian offered, lifting the counter flap, allowing Meghan to pass through under his arm. She followed Cheryl through the small kitchen to the back of the building where the exterior door opened, and the end of the diner smelled of spoiled garbage from the tall plastic trash cans that lined the outer wall under the awning.

"So, I wanted to let you know what I've been doing the last few days."

"John said he saw the lights on the police station most of the nights." Brian lit a cigarette as he talked.

Meghan nodded. She didn't know who John was, but it was no secret that she'd been working late since the murder.

"I've been on the phone a few times with Detective Gregory Anderson. He's with the Alaska State Troopers based in Anchorage." She handed Cheryl a sheet of paper with the contact information for the detective and the troopers. "He's been monitoring the flights out of town. I spoke with him yesterday, and he's sent the information about Nancy to the Fairbanks trooper branch in case there were any charter flights from town that went there. I think if any trips left here and went to Barrow, we'd know about it.

"I've done some follow-up around town and am in the process of eliminating suspects."

"You think the person who killed my sister is still in town?" Cheryl asked. She looked older, worn-down as if age caught up to her in the last few days and added a few more years to her through the bags under her eyes.

"I can't comment on that right now. When I know for sure what's going on, I will let you know. I promise."

Brian faced the two women, smoking his cigarette without added to the conversation. He looked more frustrated, almost annoyed at the whole mess.

"You determined other than the money from the cookie tin, nothing else was missing from your sister's apartment?"

"The only thing that I didn't recognize was the glove on the dresser." Cheryl had an eye for detail that Meghan liked. Maybe it was woman's intuition,

101

perhaps it was the fact that Nancy was her sister and she was protective, but the only real item that was out of the ordinary in the apartment was exactly what she brought up.

"The olive-green glove," Meghan clarified.

"It looked like something issued from the army, you know?" Brian added. He'd finished the cigarette and dug into his pocket for the pack again to light another one.

"I want you both to keep that piece of information quiet. I hope you haven't mentioned it to anyone else." The glove was a key piece of evidence. Meghan felt that the moment she saw it, photographed it, bagged it and took it back to the police department to lock in her office. She suspected the instant she saw it that it belonged to the killer. It was a crime of passion, something unplanned, unpredicted. The only piece of evidence left behind happened because someone murdered a poor girl out of spite, jealousy, or rage. That kind of crime was disorganized and often came with a string of mistakes. Robbing Nancy was an afterthought, spur of the moment following the murder. Leaving the glove behind was blind luck on Meghan's part. She hoped to get it back to Anchorage for DNA testing, but so far, the troopers weren't taking any physical evidence for the crime.

Brian and Cheryl exchanged glances. "I told my mother."

"Your mother lives in Arizona, right?"

"Yes, she talked about coming up here." Cheryl went quiet.

"She wanted us to buy her a plane ticket to come up here," Brian added. "I don't see how that's going to help anything."

"She's trying to help, Brian." Cheryl crossed over the verge of tears and had facial tissue handed, tucked into the front pocket of her apron she used to wipe her nose. "I don't even know if we can afford to bury Nancy. We don't have the money to get her cremated."

"People are putting money in her tip jar," Brian said. "It's nice, but…"

Meghan felt the tugging to avoid the family quarrel that was brewing. Using the excuse of looking at the face of her smartphone, Meghan had something else to do. "Listen, Brian; I got a problem with the starter on the Suburban, think you can take a look at it for me?"

He nodded. "We can walk around the side of the café while I finish my cigarette."

"Great, I'm parked across the street." She looked at Cheryl. Meghan wasn't a touchy-feely kind of woman. Years in the Bureau taught her to keep a professional distance from suspects and victim families. If her unit supervisor saw her getting chummy with the local newspaper reporter, he'd have shot her with a beanbag round for good measure. She rubbed her glove briefly on Cheryl's arm because the woman looked as if she was starving for physical attention. "I'll let you know if something comes up."

"Thank you, Chief."

"You're welcome, and it's Meghan." Familiarity wasn't getting familiar.

103

She stepped away from the back door of the restaurant and caught up to Brian, walking along the back of the building. Meghan sidestepped to clear the cigarette smoke that trailed after him.

Chapter Nineteen

The Suburban sat catty-corner to the restaurant. Meghan could have parked closer, but she intended to use the disabled vehicle conversation as a subterfuge. She climbed into the driver's seat, closed the door with the window down to talk to Brian.

He finished the second cigarette, snuffed it out in the gravel under the toe of the work boot. He hadn't worn a jacket outside; flannel shirt sleeves rolled up on his forearm revealed a tattoo on the inside of his arm just above the wrist. It was muted from age, a somber American flag with a silhouette of soldiers marching.

"Were you in the army?" Meghan asked. She sat in the truck because she was alone with Brian and had to talk to him about something potentially volatile and since Oliver was asleep at home because it was daytime, Lester was busy with a domestic violence call that came in that morning, and Meghan was on her own when it came to interviewing suspects.

"Coast Guard reserves," he said, lifting his arm to show off the tattoo more. He had to raise the folded sleeve to show the coast guard logo above the rest of the symbol. When he dropped his arm again, staring at Meghan through the window of the truck, he breathed through his teeth. "There's nothing wrong with your truck is there?"

"Well, it's old, got a million miles on it, and I have no idea when it had an oil change last, but no, it starts up after a while."

He looked at his boots. A few people walked by the truck, gave a friendly wave to the chief. She obliged a wave back. Then she spoke to Brian in a low tone. "I found your fingerprints on the nightstand in

Nancy's bedroom." It was enough to make his shoulders sag. "Can you tell me where you were on Friday night?"

"I was here." It came out in a flat, hard burst. Realizing what he sounded like, Brian took a few breaths. He reached for the pack of cigarettes in his pocket and lit another one. This time he breathed smoke toward the driver's side door, in Meghan's face. "I closed up around eight or nine."

"Was Nancy with you?"

"She sometimes helps, so yeah."

"After you closed the diner, did you go right home?"

"I took Nancy back to her apartment."

"Did you go inside?"

He puffed angrily on the cigarette and then rolled it between his fingers looking at the embers.

"Look, you and I both know where this is going. I can tell by your attitude that Cheryl has no idea about you having an affair with Nancy." It was out in the breezy Wednesday air and didn't hang around like the stale cigarette smoke. "I want to tell you to your face, Brian, that I'm moderately certain you didn't kill your sister-in-law."

There was shimmering under his eyes. Brian sniffled and rubbed his wrist against his eye. The end of the cigarette dropped ashes that fell like gray snowflakes.

"What happened Friday night after you took Nancy home?"

"I went upstairs with her. I do sometimes when it's late. I'll walk her to the apartment. She says the

106

neighbor down the hall sometimes peeks at her. She told me she once caught him going through her hamper in the laundry room. He had her panties when she caught him."

"Which guy is that?"

"I don't know. I think he lives in 3G."

"Do you know his name?"

"Vinnie Ackins, I think." It was close on both counts, first and last name, close enough for Meghan to have another conversation with Vincent Atkinson.

"So, Friday night," Meghan said, leading him.

"Well, you know I went inside," he said with a shrug. "Nancy always empties her tip money from the apron as soon as she gets home."

Meghan nodded. She was actively listening to Brian talk about his sister-in-law in the present tense. He knew Nancy was gone, but in his mind, at that moment, he was with her alone in the apartment.

"We were joking about the cash she had saved up. She wanted to buy a car. I thought that was a joke because she can't drive anywhere in this town." He kicked at the gravel under the driver's side door. His hand grasped the door.

"Did you sleep with Nancy?"

He didn't talk, but his body language spoke volumes. He looked up, leveling his eyes with Meghan. She swallowed because there was something dark lurking just behind those eyes. "I love Cheryl, you know? I mean, we've been together a long time. I ain't never cheated on her. But Nancy...

"She came back after her divorce, and it was like she had turned on some switch that was

107

impossible to ignore. I know Peter was an asshole. I think she married him just to get the hell out of town. But he knocked her around a couple of times. Their mother is a freak. She tried to side with Peter like it was Nancy's fault he was hitting her. She wanted Nancy to stay in Phoenix to work out their marriage."

Meghan frowned. "I thought Nancy lived in Mesa, Arizona."

"They did for a while. I think the first time Peter hit her; she ran back to mommy. Their mom lives in Phoenix now. She left Nancy with Peter in the house in Mesa."

"Okay. What happened Friday night?"

"What do you think happened?" he snapped. The tears ran free down his cheeks. They must have been cold against his skin. Brian was a conflicted man and had a lot more to worry about than icy tears. "It was just a thing. Nancy was wild, free. She married Peter and kept her last name. She knew it wasn't going to last. But she told me she felt safe with me because Cheryl felt safe with me. You know?"

Meghan stared indifferently at him. Sibling rivalry and coveting what they know was something that had been around a lot long her than the triangle between Cheryl, Brian, and Nancy. "Did Nancy have any other boyfriends in town?"

"She sometimes hinted like she was seeing other guys. She was good at flirting. I think she made about a hundred bucks a night in tips just flirting."

"Was she seeing anyone else, Brian?" she asked, "Someone that you saw her getting friendlier than anyone else?"

Brian didn't answer immediately. She saw he was working out a mental timeline, seeing Nancy flirting with other men. It seemed like a very complicated life, Brian having an affair with a woman while married to her sister, keeping it a secret in a town so small that your neighbor can hear a fart through a thin paper wall. It was way too much baggage for Meghan to comprehend.

"Are you going to tell my wife?" he asked.

This time it was Meghan who didn't talk. She bristled, and Brian saw her body language that shifted between disgust and despair.

"I didn't kill Nancy."

"I know, Brian." She felt she was right about that. He was guilty of something that he had to carry with him the rest of his life, including the fact that he had had an affair with a woman the same night someone visited her and strangled her. Meghan didn't want to consider how he would continue to get up every day after that. "I have no intention of telling your wife about you and Nancy. If it's not relevant to Nancy's death, then I'm not going to say anything. But I want you to consider this: you were the last person who saw Nancy alive. What time did you leave the apartment?"

"I left around eleven-thirty."

"Did Cheryl see you come home late?"

"No, she was in bed. I got home. I took a shower. I finished the paperwork for the day on the computer, and then I went to bed."

"What time were you on the computer?"

"After I took a shower, I think about twenty-five minutes. I put in the receipt for the day. Why?"

"The program you use is date and time stamped. If Cheryl vouches that you did the receipts, that puts you using the computer at that time."

"It's an online program we use. What about me logging on at Nancy's house."

"Did you?"

"Well, no, but I just thought..."

"Your IP at the house is good enough. If you're looking for an alibi, you don't have to. All I'm doing is covering all the ends of it. If you got something else to hide, Brian, that's on you. If you're cooking your books, I don't give a shit. If you had nothing to do with Nancy's death, that's all that matters to me. I'm not going to say a word about you and Nancy to Cheryl, but I suggest you give her a little credit. You'd be surprised what she does and doesn't know."

"You think she knows?"

Meghan started the truck. The muffler rattled against the undercarriage. Sometimes, Meghan felt like she'd gotten lost in Alaska. Then she's confronted with the same old drama that plagued the rest of the world. Dirty laundry wasn't something Meghan was any good at airing out. Now she had to deal with someone else who had a thing for dirty laundry.

Chapter Twenty

It sometimes happened during an investigation. Officers dodged between suspects, went over the covered ground, query the same people again, this time with a different set of questions. Legally, Meghan had every right to question anyone she wanted. The residents expected her to do a job that from the outside was nothing more than wandering around, talking to people casually, occasionally scolding people for riding four-wheelers or snowmachines too fast in town, and the occasional arrest for domestic violence.

Her jurisdiction didn't end when someone demanded a lawyer during questioning or denied a search of property without a warrant. While those things were important rules based on everyone's inalienable rights, what it meant for the case was any evidence collected after the individual evoked their right to refuse wasn't admissible in court for a crime.

This time when Oliver showed up at Mountain Manor, it was two in the afternoon on Wednesday. Meghan waited for him outside the truck, leaning against the fender. The break in the weather left the thick layer of ice fog but warmed up a little.

"Sorry to get you out of bed." She had a plan to follow and had specific conditions for Oliver to follow. "We're going to talk to Vincent Atkinson again. I know he's in the apartment because I went next door to the grocery store and checked with management.

The Alaska Merchandise Store was a rural example of a lower-forty-eight department store. It was the only place in town Meghan shopped. They managed the produce, dairy, and meat, and it felt like a real store with grocery carts. The company ran the franchise for years, building modern stores all over rural Alaska. It made convenient shopping, even on heavy snow days, if you could get to the store. Vincent worked in the grocery department, stocked shelves, and ran cash register when needed. He was opportunely off work when she wanted to talk to him again about his association with Nancy. It wasn't that Meghan was desperate for viable suspects; she just had no real leads to follow other than the olive-green glove and the errant fingerprint that didn't match anyone else so far.

"Listen, I know you were trying to help last time. I appreciate that. But what I'd like you to do this time is to stay back, pay attention to Vincent and me. If he has anyone in his apartment, watch them too. Be my backup, my enforcer. I want you to see how I do things. It's best if only one officer talks to a suspect at a time."

They drew a crowd again. Two police officers standing outside of any building, anywhere in America was bound to attract attention. People watched from windows, peeking through the pulled shades or around the strips of cardboard. Tenants coming and going from the complex stopped to wait and see what Meghan and her officer were doing next. She lowered her voice as they made their way into the apartment building and down the corridor.

"Whatever happens with a suspect, anyone you question, what's important is they have rights to their privacy. If you happen to catch them in the middle of something that could be embarrassing for them, you must respect them. Don't talk about it with other people. We live in a really small town, Oliver. It's bad enough everyone knows everyone else. The last thing I want is someone to think that if they talk to the cops, all their secrets are going to be public knowledge."

"Got it," he said, "Thanks, Boss."

Oliver was ambitious but needed a little fine-tuning. He hadn't gone through any police training academy. She had him and Lester complete a ton of online courses, things that were relevant to policing, but both of her officers didn't have any real-world experience. It was advantageous in some respects because they could use a go to, 'I didn't know,' and be clear of wrongdoing, as long as it wasn't extreme.

When Meghan knocked on the door for 3G, she tugged on Oliver's sleeve to pull him out of the way from standing directly in front of the door. It was an age-old tactic to stay out from in front of the door when questioning suspects. Everyone had a gun in Alaska, except the Village Public Safety Officers.

"Hey, Chief," Vincent said casually when he opened the door wearing a t-shirt, black wool socks, and basketball shorts. "Hey, Oliver," he added and wandered back into the apartment, leaving the door open for Meghan and Oliver to enter. The television was on, and the volume was up. Vincent turned down the volume but left on the TV.

"So, Vincent," Meghan started. Oliver closed the door and stood behind her as she talked to the suspect. "I wanted to talk to you about something, and it might be embarrassing, but I need to know."

The trigger word 'embarrassing' gained Meghan full attention. Vincent turned off the TV. He sat on the sofa, waiting for Meghan to continue.

"I received some information that you and Nancy had contact in the laundry room. Want to tell me about that?"

113

He waited a moment to answer. She saw him swallow, which is a physical indication that Meghan was on the right track of questioning. "Yeah, I guess."

"She caught you with her underwear." Meghan avoided using the word 'panties' because it elicited a precise response in some men who were attracted to women's undergarments, and the word was part of the lexicon for the fetish.

"Yeah, I guess."

"Want to tell me about that?" She was indifferent in her tone, balanced, unassuming. Meghan had her secrets; men and women were allowed to have secrets. As long as it didn't involve hurting others, exploiting others, didn't require a category of troubled allusions, then swiping a pair of panties wasn't going to make Meghan think less of the man; as long as it wasn't part of escalating behavior.

"I don't know."

"Well, I'm here to talk to you about what happened because before you said you saw her around, like it was just a casual thing, passing each other in the hall. I have it on good authority that you were caught going through her hamper in the laundry room." It was vague but loaded enough to prompt Vincent to stand up from the sofa.

He didn't say anything but glanced at Meghan before wandering out of the small living room. When he disappeared from view, she felt a tremor of fear because a suspect walking away from an interview is never a good thing. Meghan reached behind her, touched Oliver's chest, pushing him back toward the door. She heard Vincent opening a dresser drawer, wood scraping on wood. He was getting something in the bedroom off from the living room.

114

Since he lived in an apartment on the other side of the hall from Nancy's apartment, Meghan knew the layout, albeit, reversed from Nancy's apartment. There wasn't much cover from the small alcove where the doorway leading into the bedroom to the front door where she pushed on Oliver to back up. Meghan stood between her officer and the hallway opening. If Vincent returned flashing a weapon, she'd take the first round.

Grabbing at the pepper spray canister was impossible with the oversized coat on. She had to unzip the jacket, reach around her hip to grab the bottle attached to the basket holster on the belt. By the time she thought out it, Vincent had appeared again carrying something. It wasn't metallic.

He carried the load to the coffee table and opened his arms. Ladies undergarments fell from the basket he made with his arms. He filtered through the collection and pulled up a thong and stretched out his hand to Meghan.

Breathing again, Meghan stepped back into the living room. Oliver stood with his back to the door. She didn't know if he was scared or just shocked, he hadn't said anything or moved since she backed into him.

"What is this?" she asked.

"Those are Nancy's. I took them. I'm sorry."

Meghan focused on the rest of the collection on the table. "What about all those?" she didn't wait for him to answer. This was the warning bell ringing in her head about escalating behavior. Before she didn't care about him swiping 'a' pair, but this turned into deviant deeds. "Vincent, are these from other tenants in the building?"

115

"Yeah, I guess." He stood waiting for Meghan to scold him or arrest him or do something that put things into perspective.

She rubbed her face. "Look. Here's what's going to happen. Do you have a grocery bag?"

He nodded and moved away from the table, went into the kitchen, opened a cupboard, and pulled a bag out from under the sink.

"Put all those in there. I want Nancy's underwear on top." He did as he was told. Now she took the bag from him. "I don't have time for this Vincent. This is what I have to say: what you're doing isn't wrong; it's just a little misguided. You want panties to play with, whatever, that's fine. There are internet sites out there you can get whatever you want. Is this it?" She lifted the bag, extended to the end of her reach.

He nodded.

"No more stealing, do you understand? I can arrest you for this." She saw him tense, lip trembled. "I'm not going to arrest you, but I am going to keep an eye on you. If I get a whisper of you taking things from the laundry room, or anywhere, I will arrest you. Is that understood?"

He nodded.

"You're going to give me your fingerprints too. I want you to ride down to the police station with Oliver. We're going to get your fingerprints on file. Is that understood?"

He nodded and this time went to collect a pair of cover-alls draped over a chair. He pulled on the canvas, outerwear over the basketball shorts and

116

finished getting dressed. Meghan turned around to talk to Oliver.

"Remember what I said?"

Oliver nodded.

"He's not in too much trouble, and he doesn't need anyone knowing about this," she added, lifting the plastic grocery bag. "This is between you, me, and him. No one else. Got it?"

"I got it, Boss." The words came out coated in annoyance.

"I'm sorry, I'm not trying to treat you like a child, Oliver. I trust you. I worry about what could happen with Vincent if the wrong person found out."

"I like that you're getting his fingerprints."

She grinned at him. "See, you picked up on that. We don't have to ask him if he's been in the apartment, those prints will tell the tale."

Chapter Twenty-One

On the drive back to the police department, Meghan called Lester. The DV call lasted longer than a day. He was handling it, and she had enough confidence in him to do the right thing. But his investigation took him out of Kinguyakkii. There was a hunting camp upriver. While it was slow-going because Lester had to keep off the river because of the break-up, the shoreline was hard to transverse with the four-wheeler because some of the snow was thick in spots. The worse of it was the inability to use the cell phone to talk to him. They had to rely on the police band radio. Everyone in and around town had a scanner. Their conversations were monitored by anyone who had a two-way radio or scanner. Sometimes the police department broadcast through the radio station when they needed to boost the signal.

"K1, K2," she said into the mic.

It took a while, but Lester answered. His voice cut through the screaming wind on his end. Meghan turned down the volume. "Go ahead, K1."

"I'm checking in on you, see how it's going."

"Well, I'm almost at camp. The weather is heavy on this end of the river." That meant more bad weather was rolling in from the north. "I'm going to talk to our guy." Lester knew the radio wasn't secure. "I talked to his wife, got some pictures. I'll finish out here and talk to you later."

"Thanks, K2. Take care; be safe."

Meghan finished the call in the short time it took to drive down Third Avenue from the apartment complex. Oliver was coming shortly with Vincent to fingerprint.

She unlocked the front door and went inside.

"What the hell are you doing?" she asked when she saw Duane standing at her office door with a large ring of keys in his hand. He was in the middle of trying each of the keys on the locked door. Meghan knew he didn't have a key because she'd ordered replacement doorknobs for the office on her second day as chief of police. He didn't know that or need to know she'd replaced the locks.

"You can't keep this door locked. What if I have to get in there?" Duane was a little startled when Meghan unlocked the front door to the station. He had that 'oops, you caught me,' look that wasn't going away because it morphed into a mask of irritation.

Meghan approached Duane, crossing through the small gate, moving by the Formica table, and stood, so Duane had to turn away from the office door to face her. She wasn't in the mood. Whatever agenda he had was just a nuisance for her. Meghan wasn't giving in to his bullying.

"This is town property." He had an argument for her prepared, and it sounded as if Duane rehearsed the lines. "Your authority here doesn't include you shutting me out of the day to day business running this city. I have over four thousand people—"

"Three thousand," Meghan corrected Duane's embellishment. "There're three thousand, well a little less, in the city." It was a passive-aggressive maneuver to make him stumble in the prepared speech. "What does you being mayor have to do with getting into my office?"

"I need the recent financial reports."

"I'll submit them at the end of the week, just like I always do." She narrowed her eyes accusingly at him. "What's really going on around here Duane? I feel like ever since I started this investigation, you've been riding on my heels."

"This isn't your investigation. I called the Alaska State Troopers, they said—"

"They? Who did you talk to, Duane? What was the person's name? What department were 'they' in; did you explain your chief of police already submitted all the information regarding the murder?" She shook her head. It wasn't Meghan's best hour. She wasn't in the business of confrontation when it came to petty power plays, but Duane irked her, and she felt inclined to push back. "Who did you speak with? I need to know to make sure I send another follow-up email to the detective in charge."

"I didn't get a name but—"

Meghan looked to the front reception area. They were alone in the building. While she'd left the door unlocked, if anyone came in, they'd see the person through the archway. "Help me, Duane, stop getting in my way. You knew Nancy, everyone in town knew her. If you care so much for the residents of Kinguyakkii, you'd be glad that I give a shit about her too.

"I get everyone sees me as an outsider. Anyone who wasn't born in Alaska or hasn't been here for twenty years is an 'outsider.' I don't care, what I care about is someone put their hands around that girl's neck and choked her hard enough to crush a tiny little bone designed to keep you breathing and your tongue from falling back into your throat. It's a god-awful way to die, Duane, and someone got away with it." She gave him more than enough to chew on, and it appeared the small sliver of detailed description worked on him. He sidestepped from the front of the office door. Meghan didn't unlock it.

"Whatever this is," she said, moving her hands between them as a physical representation of the riff. "It needs to stop. I'm doing the job I was hired to do. I don't know why it's a problem."

Oliver and Vincent walked through the front door. Oliver showed Vincent through the back. The look on Oliver's face suggested he knew something happened between Duane and his chief.

"Oliver, this is a good opportunity to learn how to fingerprint people." Meghan dropped the plastic bag by the office door on the floor. She saw Duane lean over to look inside. The floral and frilly prints of various materials jumbled together showed and he knew what was in the bag as his eyes darted back to Meghan. "It's my laundry day," she said and left it alone.

Ignoring Duane, Meghan joined Oliver and Vincent on the other side of the large table in the main room. Duane moved toward the door, glancing over his shoulder as he left. Meghan shed her heavy coat, dropped it on the table. Oliver and Vincent followed suit.

"Vincent, we need you to go wash your hands before we start." She looked at Duane standing under the archway near the front. "Is there anything else I can get you, Mayor?"

He left, slamming the door behind him.

She collected the small digital scanner bed with finger grooves. It was part of the kit she'd ordered from Quantico and Meghan wasn't going to make any part of it available to the public. Keeping the office door locked kept things secure; the evidence was stacked on a small side table in her office. Fingerprint cards, clear plastic bags of physical evidence, including the cookie tin and the olive-green army glove, all gathered and stored under the table. Meghan didn't want to think that Duane needed to get into the office other than his controlling issues.

The relationship he had with the former chief of police was very close. When Alaska State Trooper arrested the former chief for conspiracy to commit crimes, tampering with evidence, and bootlegging, Meghan had a very long conversation with the ATF agents in charge of this tiny dark corner of the world. Duane Warren was in their sights as part of the operation. He was cleared because there was no evidence linking him to the chief and the former chief wasn't rolling over on anyone who may have helped.

Meghan felt Duane was a little misguided, a little high-strung, and impatient with anything outside his control. She thought he wasn't a criminal and deep down he cared for the city. Whatever his reason for trying to get into her office, Meghan hoped it had nothing to do with the investigation.

Chapter Twenty-Two

Lester stayed at the camp overnight. The ice fog condensed and lay suspended in the windless air. Once the delicate ice crystals rolled into town, it was as if the precipitation was too thick to move out again without the help of wind gusts pushing across the tundra. Encrusted in icy frosting, the sunlight had diminished, unable to break through the fog. The ambient temperature dropped again, and while people were saying it wasn't going to snow again, the conditions were right. Smaller planes were grounded. Communication on the two-way radio with her officer alone in the wild was spotty.

His confidence in the group of hunters he was with ensured Meghan that Lester was distinct by himself. VPSOs weren't allowed firearms within the town limits. However, as a precaution, heading into the feral landscape of the Alaska tundra, guns were a necessity. Lester had a rifle with him for personal protection. That made Meghan more comfortable with his decision to stay until daybreak before heading back the twenty-something miles along the shoreline.

Oliver went home, was on-call for police business, which meant he'd handle most calls over the phone, take notes, and if Meghan felt the overnight calls needed a follow-up, she'd do it in the morning. Noise complaints and other petty issues weren't something people usually called the police about. If a bear wandered into the village, someone would report it. Other than another emergency, Oliver would stay home, watch TV, and go to bed unless he was needed.

At home, away from the police department, Meghan sat on the couch with the television on for background noise. She sat cross-legged on the sofa, reading over the case log she'd put together on

Nancy's death. She'd done everything in her power, used all the tools available at her disposal, and someone still got away with murder.

It was after eleven, and the surrounding houses were dark. The town had a smattering of streetlights that populated some of the intersection corners, but none near the small house she had rented.

There were still moving boxes tucked against the wall in the corner of the dining room: books, photo albums, things she didn't need immediately once Meghan moved to Kinguyakkii. Now the stack of cardboard boxes was storage, put on the permanent to do list that she'd never get done. Months later, they were part of the furniture. Now Meghan felt with the tension between her and Duane; the man would find a way to convince the borough council to get rid of her. If Duane could pinch coal long enough to make diamonds he would. Meghan had blown the planned budget for the department on equipment she felt necessary to do her job. Only Duane made her feel as if whatever she did wasn't in the best interest of the city.

The smartphone rang, and Meghan saw Oliver's grinning face for the contact. "What's up?"

"Hey Boss, are you working at the office?"

"No, I'm home now. Why?"

"I got a call from Valerie and Tom Harper, and they were driving by the police station, said the light was on in the office." Tom worked for the town transformer plant. He was diligent about town officials burning unnecessary electricity. The past few nights Meghan worked late were followed up companywide emails regarding turning off lights to conserve energy.

124

Kinguyakkii was on an independent power source. Enormous free-standing diesel generators powered the whole city. They were lucky to have modern conveniences light electricity, internet, limited cell phone range, and most importantly, plumbing and sewage. Meghan visited a few of the outlying villages from time to time for calls, and some people had was what they referred to as "honey pots" in their homes or very close by, fifty-five gallon drums used for toilet needs. The stench wasn't close to honey.

"I thought I turned off the lights." Meghan uncoiled her legs from under her on the cushion and stood up. Her knees popped.

"I can go shut off the lights."

"No, Oliver, I'll go. It's my fault. Thanks anyway."

***

The hush across the town was pleasant. It was cold but not the 'take your breath away' bitter that sometimes happened when stepping outside. It was March, and the sun did its best to warm the landscape. Except the ice fog gripped the town and made it hard to see the edges of the road.

Instead of driving the Suburban to the police station and back home again, Meghan bundled up in her oversized parka, put on gloves, ski cap, and the ivory bunny boots. She needed to get more exercise. Every time Meghan pulled on her jeans, the button-fly front took increasingly more time and longer breaths to hold when she fastened the pants. A little nighttime walking helped work off the fast-food and winter drag on her boot heels.

From the house, walking along Bison street to the intersection of Third Avenue, it was another half-

125

mile at the most, took close enough to burn up more fuel when it was a simple turnaround.

The pale siding of the contractor trailers was hard to see through the thick white soup in the air. Streetlights on the corners cast a pasty glow over the immediate area, unable to cut through the ice crystals. The ruddiness of the office light inside the police station looked more like a small candle in the window. Leave it to Tom to pick out that light driving by the office.

Like most buildings, the trailers had two entrances. Meghan commonly used the central, front porch. The side access was higher off the ground, taller steps leading to the single door. They stored pallets near the side door, creating a breaker from the wind that cut through the town sometimes like a razor-sharp knife. There was a wooden bin for the garbage cans from the department near the side entrance. It was easier to enter through the side than the front when she walked across the gravel yards between the buildings.

At the door, Meghan paused. The tiny window in the door showed the Formica table and the office on the other side of the trailer. The door was open, light on, and as Meghan slowly, quietly slipped the key into the doorknob lock, she saw a figure moving around inside her office.

The small hallway to the side door had the bathroom on the left when she entered. She'd arrived without a canister of pepper spray because she hadn't bothered putting on the uniform to turn off lights. Meghan wasn't expecting to see someone had broken into the police station and her office.

126

The figure switched off the light in the office, dousing the rest of the interior in blackness. Meghan reached the far side of the Formica table, managed to get her hand on a plastic formed chair before the light went out.

That moment of instant blackness, when all light stops, and the eyes can't adjust left Meghan blinded for a few seconds. She used the memory of space to lift the chair and hurtle it across the table toward where she suspected the burglar moved.

"Hey!" she yelled, running in the dark, knocking her thigh against the table, arms flailing.

The figure tripped over the chair Meghan threw in the path, fell toward the archway. It was a man; she'd heard his "oomph," as he fell over the throne chair. He was agile, on his feet and the moment he burst through the small gate and out the front door, Meghan closed the space, limping after him.

By the time she reached the top step, peering outside, the icy fog had devoured the running man. It was pointless to pursue.

Instead, Meghan turned on the rest of the lights inside the station and returned to the office.

The limited collection of evidence was missing. Her box of homemade fingerprint samples was gone, the olive-green glove, the cookie tin, everything she'd assembled was missing. When the man fell, a few packing tape fingerprint cards spilled on the floor by the archway.

Meghan dropped in the chair she'd thrown at the suspect after she turned it upright. Sitting in the main room of the department, rubbing her thigh, she thought what to do next. He got the evidence without vandalism. If he was dressed for cold weather, he

127

wore gloves. She knew he had on a ski mask because there was only the shape of a head in the room before the light went out, no hair, and no flesh showing.

Exhaling in frustration, Meghan stood up and limped to the office door. The lock was jimmied, pulled apart from the aluminum doorframe where the latch mechanism held the door locked. The police laptop was still on the desk. The burglar got the fingerprint cards but didn't know about the software program that made the card redundant because she had a digital collection. Meghan thought if he was after something, the prints were a bonus, she suspected it was the army glove that he wanted. Now he had the glove, the one real piece of evidence leftover from a senseless murder of a misguided woman who hadn't quite figured out her lift, now she never would.

Meghan picked up the few pieces of debris left over from the new crime scene. She pulled the smartphone from the deep well pocket on the oversized coat and began taking pictures of the scene. A digital camera was the next big purchase for the department.

Chapter Twenty-Three

Since the night was ruined, Meghan didn't get any sleep. She spent the remaining time alone at the department. First, she documented the damage, took pictures, and looked for leftover clues, nothing valuable in the detritus. Then came the cleaning, starting with her office. It needed a good scrubbing anyway, and since there was a utility closet full of cleaning supplies, Meghan dusted, scrubbed, and vacuumed the entire department. She found some air fresheners and placed them around.

By the time Oliver showed up for work, the coffee was ready, and the place was spotless.

"What happened?" he asked, seeing the crisp tabletops, the straightened chairs, and lack of clutter from available surfaces. Even the small kitchenette, where everyone used the microwave, but no one ever cleaned it, was spotless.

"I got bored." Meghan took a few ibuprofen for the pain and swelling of her leg. She sat at her desk, finishing the incident report from the night before. Meghan made a copy for the Alaska State Troopers and emailed it to Detective Anderson, and cc'd Duane. She wanted to make it look official. Nonetheless, two incidents of breaking into her office were hard to separate into coincidences.

"What happened to your office door?" Oliver was observant. He was younger, and some people thought he was a little slow on the uptake, but Meghan learned he used the outside observation as an advantage, people took him for granted. They underestimated his abilities. Meghan had a proper officer.

"Well, that's from when someone broke into the station last night and took our evidence."

Oliver stood within the doorframe facing her, absorbing the information. "So, Tom saw the light on, and that wasn't you, it was someone stealing the stuff?"

"That's right."

"Who would steal tape and a cookie jar?"

"Someone who committed murder and wanted to keep it secret," Meghan said. "Or someone who knows who the killer is and wants to keep it secret. Or someone who wants to keep something secret but wasn't the killer."

"That's a lot to unpack, Boss."

"You're telling me."

Oliver retreated to the main room, circled the table and went to fix himself a cup of coffee. "It's clean in here, smells nice too."

"Thanks," she called from the desk in the office.

Oliver returned to the office, leaning against the now-defunct doorjamb. "Did Lester get a hold of you this morning?"

"No, you hear from him?"

"I got a call from a friend who came in this morning from camp. He was out there when Lester was talking to Billy." Billy Tate was the domestic violence suspect. He left town shortly after smacking his wife, Jessie. Small town drama that needed dealing with and no place to put the bad guys. "Billy ain't going to hit Jessie anymore."

"So, he says," she mumbled. In the real world, Billy would be in jail. In rural Alaska, the incident was documented, Meghan would follow up with Jessie, try to get the woman some hotline numbers she could call for support. Lester would work up the report, submit it to the local magistrate, and while they had a limited justice system, if the court saw fit to reprimand Billy, he'd go willingly if needed.

"What you going to do about the break-in?"

"Not sure what I can do." She sat back in the chair that squeaked whenever she moved in it. "I documented everything. I'm going to take home the department laptop, or maybe if you're working nights, you keep it at your apartment. You'd think the police department would be a safe place to keep stuff."

She stood, stretched, feeling exhaustion pull at her limbs. Meghan put on her coat, stepped back into the bunny boots, and gave Oliver a look of endearment. "Can I borrow the Polaris? I left the Suburban at the house last night."

Oliver put the keys on the counter as he settled in the reception chair. "It's the department four-wheeler, Boss. You don't have to ask."

"I'm asking, Oliver, because you are a skilled officer who will be without a vehicle in case you have to race to a call and save a life."

Oliver chuckled. "Your patronizing ain't going to bother me."

Meghan clapped him on the shoulder, collected the keys to the Polaris, and limped out the front door. "You should go to the clinic."

"It's not that bad. If it turns green, I'll go to the clinic. Waiting at the top of the stairs, watching Oliver at the front counter, she asked, "When is Lester coming back?"

He shrugged an answer. Somehow Oliver had shifted to days without being asked. It was some natural system the two of them worked out. Cousins, they had limited similarities, other than Inuit features, both men worked on a level of the subconscious that baffled Meghan. If they had worked out the schedule changes without informing Meghan, that was perfectly acceptable. She wasn't a micromanager; no one needed that kind of shadow.

"I'm heading over to the apartment complex. You need anything, call me. If the guy that broke into this place last night happens to show up again, sit on him until I get back."

"You got it, Boss."

Meghan swung her leg over the seat of the Polaris. Most people in the village rode four-wheelers year around. It was cost-effective and with limited roadways, better than owning a car. Any vehicle brought to the town never left. Skeletal remains of broken-down cars littered much of the city's landscape. It was an unfortunate castoff of a mechanized society. People were getting better at taking care of their equipment, but every year, one or two people thought to leave an abandoned truck, snowmachine, or car along the winding road that looped around the town in an eight-mile ring was a better idea than neglecting it to rust next to their houses. It took time, but people were starting to catch up. It helped that Meghan had every vehicle in the town registered with the police department.

Chapter Twenty-Four

Before Meghan pulled up to Mountain Manor, she acclimated herself with the Polaris. The four-wheeler had seen some rough winters and some unkind hands before the town purchased it and it was eventually passed down to the police department. Lester and Oliver took care of the machines and did what they could with a limited budget. Much of the four-wheeler was held together by duct tape, a standby tool in the north. Duct tape was part of any survival kit in Alaska. There were a few small planes on the airstrip with pieces and parts secured with industrial tape.

She drove at a reasonable speed, around twenty miles per hour to keep the chill from tearing the hood off her head. It was daylight somewhere above that low ceiling of fog that continued to hold over the town like an unyielding white haze. Meghan pulled around the multiunit building, driving along the side, around back, front, and to the side again where she stopped at the exit closest to the stairwell and Nancy's apartment. Sitting on the Polaris, waiting to go inside, she considered what was lost and if the culprit had done anything more to Nancy's apartment after or before he decided to rob the police station.

"Howdy, Sheriff!" someone called to her from the road. There were a group of twenty-something adults moving along the roadway, huddled together and headed for the Alaska Merchandise Store.

Rather than correct them, seeing the group were giggling after the waving, Meghan climbed off the four-wheeler saddle with a returned wave and wandered toward the apartments.

There were no CCTV cameras anywhere in town, no security on the building. People came and went as they wanted or needed. She made her way inside the side door closest to the stairwell and stood in the hallway.

Music and television noise filled the space, along with cigarettes and a hint of marijuana smoke. She looked at each of the first-floor doors down the hallway. To her left, the apartment closest to the stairwell, there was something on the door that made Meghan's heart skip.

She reached out and pushed the button on the electronic doorbell. It was a smart doorbell. Meghan watched the little camera on the device and removed her hood, pulled at the zipper on her coat. The temperature inside the apartment building was stifling.

There was a rattle of locks, and the door popped open. "Hello, Ma'am, my name's Meghan Sheppard."

"Hello, Chief," the old woman said. Wearing the town police uniform under the coat spoke volumes for people who she didn't know. "What can I do for you?" She was an elder, weathered, and bent from the cold climate. She used a quad prong cane to hobble around.

"Ma'am, I am curious about your doorbell here." Meghan pointed because the older woman seemed not quite to understand what she meant until she followed Meghan's finger to the small device attached to the doorjamb.

"Oh, yes, my son installed that," she said and backed up because turning around seemed harder on her hips. "Please, come in."

134

Stepping over the threshold of the apartment, she was struck by the scent of cinnamon and lavender. While it appeared, the elderly woman wasn't as mobile as she once was, the apartment was sparse and spotless. Meghan stood on the floor mat by the door. Most of the time, no one wore boots inside their homes. It was out of respect that she unlaced and pulled off the bunny boots before following the woman further into the apartment.

It was a mirror opposite of Nancy's apartment, one bedroom.

"Ma'am, about your doorbell," she started again.

"My son, Jeff, he installed that, and I guess it's supposed to keep an eye on me." She moved around, Meghan into the kitchen. "I don't understand it myself. He lives in Anchorage. He tells me he can see who comes to my place." She removed a plastic container from the refrigerator, pulled two small bowls from the dish strainer in the sink. Meghan watched as the old woman scooped what looked like thick whipped cream with berries mixed in it.

She removed two coffee cups from the cupboard. After they were set out on the counter, the elder poured two cups of coffee from the pot cradled in the maker. She handed Meghan a cup, a spoon, and the bowl of creamy white frosting with blueberries and raspberries mixed in.

Meghan carried the bowl and the coffee to the tiny two-chair table off from the kitchen.

"This is Akutaq," she said. "You call it Eskimo Ice Cream. It took the elder a moment to settle in the chair. The four-prong cane stood idle once she sat down. "Please, sit." She sipped at the coffee. Either the old woman lost her bottom teeth or wasn't

135

wearing her dentures. Her chin poked out from under her small round nose. She grinned at Meghan with minimal teeth.

Meghan sat down after she removed the coat and draped it over the chair.

"Now, I make Akutaq a little different than most. I use a lot of sugar. I like sugar. It's not traditional to the recipe, but it's good, right?"

Obligated to taste it, Meghan dipped the spoon tip into the bluish, red thick cream. There was a hint of seal oil from the mix. She found it impossible to describe the scent of seal oil. The closest she could muster was ammonia and decomposing fish. Tasting the mix without breathing, Meghan smiled, nodding, and washed down the mess with a quick gulp of coffee.

"So, the doorbell, you said your son, Jeff got it for you."

"Yes, he says he can see when I come and go. He says he can see when I have visitors. He sometimes calls when—" The house phone rang. Unlike most people in town, the old woman still had a landline instead of a smartphone. "That's probably Jeff. Could you get that for me, Dear?" she asked.

Meghan stood up, went to the small stand by the hallway leading to the bedroom, and picked up the wireless phone. She handed it to the woman.

"Ah, hello?" The woman grinned and nodded. "Yes, Son, no—no, everything is okay. The police chief is here. No, she didn't tell me why she's here."

Meghan felt a burst of embarrassment because here she was, boots off, making herself to home in a stranger's house, having coffee and something that's

136

supposed to resemble dessert, and she didn't even know the lady's name.

"Why don't I have you talk to her, Jeffrey?" She handed the phone to Meghan.

"This is Chief Sheppard."

"Is everything okay? Is my mother okay?"

"Yes, is this Jeff?"

"Yes, Jeffrey Ravenswaay, my mother is Andrea Ravenswaay."

"Mr. Ravenswaay," she started.

"Jeff."

"Meghan." Formalities out of the way, Meghan felt she was communicating with someone who understood the electronic age. "Listen, I'm not sure if you're aware of what happened Saturday—"

"Nancy McCormick was murdered."

"Yes, that's why I'm here today. Your mother has a smart doorbell."

"I live in Anchorage. It's the only way I can keep an eye on her. When I heard about Nancy, I was ready to call you to find out if you caught the guy." It was a generalization, Meghan knew. Most murders, especially when a woman was the victim, had to do with a male suspect.

"We're working on it. We're doing some follow-up, and I saw the doorbell, so here I am."

"I'm not sure if it's going to be much help to you. What are you looking for?"

"Does it record people moving by the apartment as well as ringing the doorbell?"

"It's motion activated. I've had to modify the range because people are always using the door by my mom's place."

"Do you store the data?"

"It's on automatic dump after the cache is full. I don't know if I'd have anything from more than a few days. What are you looking for?"

"I'm curious if you have any images from Saturday night."

Jeff sucked air through his teeth before he answered. "That's a while. I'd have to check to see if the memory deleted."

"I understand. We're just tying up loose ends."

"Did you get the guy?" he asked hurriedly.

"I'm sorry, Jeffrey." She was pleasant about him asking. Everyone wanted to know. "I can't comment on an ongoing investigation."

"That's cop-speak for shut up, right?" He laughed.

"Not at all." Meghan felt better about their communication. She gave Jeff her town email address. She had him read it back to her, so he copied it right. "If you find anything from the camera system, I would appreciate it."

"I'll check tonight when I get home from work."

"Thank you."

"Is my mom okay there?"

"She's fine." Meghan smiled at Andrea. The old woman spooned the last of the Akutaq into her toothless mouth.

"I worry about her. I'm really worried about what happened to Nancy."

"Well, it's been a long time since that happened. I think everything is okay with your mother. I'll keep an eye on her for you."

"Thank you, Meghan."

"Did you want to talk to her again?"

"No, if she gets the phone, she'll never hang up with me. Good luck trying to get out of her apartment. She's chatty. And if she offers you any Akutaq just say 'no, thank you,' I think she's still using a jar of seal oil from last year."

"I'll keep that in mind. Thank you."

"Hey, you don't see any old containers on her counters in the kitchen, do you?" The question made Meghan curious and peered around the counter space for something that resembled what Jeff described.

"I don't see anything, why?"

"My mother is notorious for digging up old jars of 'stinky heads' around the outskirts of town."

"I'm not sure what that means," Meghan admitted.

Jeffery chuckled. "I forget you are kind of new to town. It's fermented fish heads and salmon eggs. My mother will go out and find jars that her mother buried in the tundra. It's a big nasty mess of poison. Most of the time, it causes botulism."

"Oh, boy," Meghan said. She looked a little hard for old jars that might have recently been unearthed.

"Yeah, the elders still eat that crap, my mother included."

139

"I don't see anything like that in her apartment."

"Thanks for looking."

"Thank you for getting those data files."

"I hope they work for you. Bye, Meghan." Jeffery ended the call, and Meghan returned the phone to the charging stand.

"He had to go?" Andrea asked.

"Yes, sorry, Mrs. Ravenswaay. And I have to get going too." Meghan went to the door and slipped on her boots. When she grabbed her coat from the back of the chair, she asked Andrea, "You don't happen to have any jars of *stinky fish*, do you?"

The old lady smiled at Meghan.

Chapter Twenty-Five

When Meghan returned to the police department, Oliver looked up from an issue of *Northern Lights Sounder*. Most of the time the newspaper came out on Fridays, sometimes didn't ship into town from the newspaper press in Anchorage until Saturday or Sunday. Either Oliver had an old issue, or Calvin went to press early.

"What's that?" he asked.

Carefully, Meghan lifted the glass Mason jar and placed it on the counter. "That is Andrea Ravenswaay's latest jar of 'stinky fish.'"

Oliver's eyes went wide. He leaned away from the front desk. "That stuff can make you real sick."

"I know. Andrea was nice enough to relinquish it without a fight. She thinks I took it home to eat it."

"What are you going to do with it?"

"Well, I was hoping you could do something with it."

"Should go bury it again," he stated and stood up. Oliver followed Meghan into the main room to collect his jacket from the coat rack. "I can take it to the dump. If it breaks open out there at least, no one will smell it. Might even scare away the wolverines in the dump," he said.

"I was worried about it breaking open on the ride back here. Be careful with it."

"The mayor came by to see you."

"Did he say what he wanted?"

Oliver shook his head. "He saw the door to the office was busted. I told him what happened. He was mad, started yelling, and left. I think he went to call the troopers or something."

"He can call the governor for all I care." The door had to be repaired, and since the frame was twisted, it wasn't going to be a cheap fix. "At least now he can't complain about getting into the office." Oliver got as far as the front door before Meghan raised her voice from the back. "Did Lester check in?"

"Yeah," Oliver said. "He's on his way back. He said it was slow going because some of the river was running free and overflowed. He might be back after nightfall."

"Thanks for covering for me today. I'll take the calls tonight. You can have a night off."

"Thanks, Boss."

Nightfall in March happened after nine now; each day, they gained another seven to fourteen minutes of daylight. That meant another long day for Lester. The Polaris sputtered to life outside when Oliver rode off with the lethal fish brew. The town dump was two miles out of town, downwind.

In the quiet of the building, Meghan went to her office and looked at what she had to work with since the robbery. Dropping in the squeaky chair, Meghan sighed. Once she thought to be an FBI Agent was a kickass job. When her career ended with a bullet, becoming the chief of police, almost five thousand miles away seemed like a safe way to spend her retirement.

Now Meghan felt like a failure because she didn't have the proper tools or human resources to do the job. That was before she lost the evidence. If Jeffery's smart doorbell caught the killer exiting the apartment

142

building, provided the killer went out the side door, Meghan might get the redemption she needed.

The desk had manila files. Case reports from the week collected. She was supposed to review everything, initial it, and log it. Once she opened the department laptop, Meghan realized Oliver was supposed to take it with him but forgot. Her computer was at the house and hopefully, the person who broke into the office last night wasn't in the mood to steal from her home that night.

She checked the department email. There was a priority email from Duane that Meghan immediately deleted before reading. Whatever he had to say could be done face to face. She read an email from Detective Anderson. He had nothing to contribute to the case, asked when she was ready to list it as a cold case so he could file it with the state trooper case logs.

Why was everyone willing to give up so easily? She wondered. Meghan sent a reply email that included an attachment to the incident report from the burglary. She took pictures with her phone and attached the photographs to the email. Meghan wasn't ready to let go of the case.

To her right was a stack of overdue notices Nickolas Hodge handed Meghan the day she visited him at the office. She let out a heavy sigh and grabbed the stack of warnings. Before she put the papers in front of her, Meghan saw how she held onto the stack—four fingers toward the end of the sheet, thumb on the top. Immediately, Meghan dropped the notices and got up from the desk.

***

The fingerprint kit Meghan ordered from the FBI was one she learned to collect prints with. It took no time at all to dust the papers for latent fingerprints. Why not have a set from Hodge? Meghan wanted fingerprints from Duane too; she had to figure out how to get them without him noticing.

In a stroke of genius, Meghan got up from the desk and ran across the main room, around the Formica table. In the trashcan out the side door was a leftover pizza box Calvin brought with him the last night she saw him.

It only took ten minutes to pull latent fingerprints from the pizza box. She'd handled the box twice, once to throw it away, once to retrieve it. Only she and Calvin's prints were on the box. Meghan fed the fingerprints into the scanner bed.

Once she had clear prints from the papers Hodge had printed for her and handed off, Meghan scanned the images into the software program. Hodge was right-handed. He handled the late notices with his left hand, pulling them off the printer, collating them on his desk, before handing them to Meghan with his right hand. She remembered watching him but hadn't thought anything of it until that moment while the software program scanned each of the prints to match them against the one copy collected from the dresser.

The forensic science of fingerprint collection and analysis has been around since the late 1700s. It wasn't until Juan Vucetich, and Inspector Alvarez of an Argentine police department used the first police collected fingerprints to convict a woman of killing her two children, trying to blame a neighbor for the crime, when her prints were collected from the knife, she used to murder the children. Back then, the composition of the fingerprint powder wasn't most different than Meghan used to manage the prints in Nancy's apartment. The fingerprints on the overdue rent notices from Blue Sky Realty were crisp and refined because the stuff Meghan got from the FBI was the best.

She sat back, watching the computer screen as the program went through the analysis. After a few minutes, yawning and rubbing her face, the program grabbed at the exemplar prints she had on file and matched them to the focused latent prints.

The laptop chirped an audio alarm that alerted Meghan she had a possible match. The software program declared a match when the friction ridge impressions wavered between twelve and twenty points. Side by side comparison of the prints highlighted the loops and whorls consistent between the two images. There was consistency between the arches as well.

Meghan had a final match for the fingerprint.

It took her a moment before she realized that in her haste to input two more suspect's fingerprints, she hadn't labeled the prints. From the pizza box, she entered five good copies. From the Blue Sky Realty paperwork, she had three good prints. Out of the eight fingerprint comparisons, one was a match to the print collected on the dresser in Nancy's apartment.

Meghan pulled the smartphone from her coat pocket and tapped in Oliver's contact.

"Hel—this—liver."

"Oliver? Can you hear me? Are you still at the dump?"

"—ey, Boss, I—flat—back."

"Sorry?" Meghan plugged her opposite ear with her finger and listened harder. "I can't understand you. Are you still at the dump? Did you get a flat tire?"

"Yeah—brok—glass. I—alking, back."

"I think you said you were walking back."

"Yeah—" the call ended. One thing about the limited range of cell phones in the bush, they had one cell tower, mounted near the airport. It was barely in the line of sight from the airfield.

Megan called Lester, and the phone went to voicemail. She was on her own.

Chapter Twenty-Six

While it wasn't the best circumstance when it came to apprehending a suspect, Meghan had more experience than both Lester and Oliver. Kinguyakkii was in the middle of nowhere, but there were a million ways out of town and anyone on the run, if they knew how to survive in the wild, they might get away with murder.

She was on foot, cursing and running toward the other side of town. It was nearly impossible to run with bunny boots on, and after a few hundred yards, thighs burning, Meghan slowed to a brisk walk.

When she reached the *Northern Lights Sounder* office, Meghan suspected no one was home. Balled fist, banging against the door, she waited, panting from the exertion. Meghan resolved than when this was all over, and she needed to get back into shape. She doubled-down and banged on the door to the trailer again. All the lights were off, Calvin was nowhere in sight, and his vehicle was missing. Standing outside the trailer, Meghan has to make a decision. She was the chief of police, had a responsibility to do the right thing. Calvin was missing, somewhere doing whatever it was reporters did when they weren't flirting with the police chief or writing articles for a rural Alaska newspaper.

***

Meghan swore again as she hopped off the steel steps and hurried along the road, cutting through the tall brown scrub brush, thistles, and Loosestrife. No one had lawns in Kinguyakkii. Most of the time it was wild bracken and gravel when snow didn't blanket the ground, with summer coming, snowmelt gave way to muddy patches of land. She wanted to approach the residence from the back instead of the road. It had more cover, no light from the streetlamp, and as she got closer, she saw a light on inside the house.

Pausing at the rear corner of the house, Meghan felt the hammering in her chest. She was alone, no backup, and from the look of the home, Nickolas Hodge already left. He could be anywhere.

The backdoor had a screen door and an interior door. When Meghan opened the screen door, the piston closer hissed, but the hinges were quiet. The interior doorknob was unlocked. She turned it all the way to the right and pushed. The wooden door had swelled from the inside heat and the outside moisture. The uneven linoleum floor scraped against the bottom of the door, stopping it from swinging open cleanly. The door stopped too close for her to slip inside. Meghan exhaled quietly and pressed her shoulder against the door, using her weight to open it, holding the doorknob as leverage.

The bottom of the door scraped the linoleum. Wood on plastic sounded like an artificial fart and Meghan knew it was loud enough to hear through the whole house.

The back of the house was mostly the kitchen. There was a pantry to her left, the counter, appliances, and a thin walkway that made up the rest of the cooking space. She saw one light on in the living room. It was a single-story house with very few places to hide. If Nickolas wasn't in the living room, he was either in the bathroom or bedroom; if he hadn't fled town.

Meghan reached for the light switch. When the figure appeared at the doorway to the living room, it was backlit by the light from the living room. It didn't

148

wait for Meghan to pull the canister of pepper spray from her holster. It lunged at her.

Nickolas was younger, taller, and when he tackled Meghan, she realized he was stronger than he looked. The oversized winter coat, a parka that was two sizes bigger than her frame, seemed like a good idea to keep warm. While it cushioned Meghan as she slammed against the kitchen counter, she realized the added layer of material put her inside a cocoon, practically gift wrapped for Nickolas.

She hit the counter. Nickolas growled in her ear as his long arms wrapped around her and heaved. Her feet left the floor, boots up; she was freefalling backward, slung like a ragdoll. This time her shoulder and head banged against the pantry door; the wood splintered as she saw a flash of white. Meghan fell forward, trying to catch herself. Canned goods rained down on her from the shelves. The broken door crashed to the floor beside her.

Nickolas meant to kick her in the side. She saw the foot come up and managed to twist away. He wasn't wearing shoes and the socked foot connected with the baseboard. Nickolas yelped and dropped his weight on Meghan. She elbowed him, but the coat sleeve padded his face against a good hit. Nickolas grunted, yanking on the inside hook of her arm to turn her over and put his weight on Meghan's middle. He bore down on her. Before she could react, fight off his pressure, Nickolas' hands reached for her throat.

It was impossible to see his face clearly. Too dark in the kitchen, the hood of the oversized parka obscured most of her view. She felt and smelt his heated breath on her face as his fingers closed around her thin neck. He'd done it before. This is what Nancy felt when Nickolas squeezed the life out of her. This is

149

a scenario Meghan had trained for during her hand to hand combat with the FBI. Real life was never like simulation. Her sparring partner went easy on her. Nickolas had taken a life once; he had no qualms about doing it again.

Meghan pulled at the thumb on Nickolas' right hand against her neck. As the pressure increased, if she could get her fist around the digit, she could break his thumb, her nails scratched against her throat, pulling at the thumb that felt like fleshy stone.

In desperation, as panic blinded her, Meghan's right hand closed around a jar that had fallen to the floor from the pantry. She grabbed the plastic pot and swung her arm up.

The plastic container smashed against Nickolas' face. His hands relented on her throat, and Meghan sucked in a massive gulp of air. The lid of the plastic jar shattered when Meghan knocked Nickolas off. He arched back, hands off her throat but still sitting on her middle. Meghan squeezed the jar and swung again. This time whatever was inside the plastic jar squeezed out. Meghan caught a whiff of peanut butter. A gob of putty smeared over her fingers. She hit Nickolas against in the face a third time.

Something happened. His hands went to his throat, and Nickolas gasped for air as he tilted sideways, and Meghan kicked out from under him.

She scrambled away from him, dropped the peanut butter jar, and saw his shape on the floor in the kitchen as Nickolas gagged, rolled on his side and wheezed. Meghan rolled and crawled away from him, using his injury to her advantage. There was a switch on the wall. She reached for it, smearing peanut butter against the wall.

The overhead fluorescent light flickered on in the kitchen. Lying on the floor in a fetal position, Nickolas clutched at his throat, gasping for air. There was no apparent injury. There was no visible damage to his face other than gobs of creamy peanut butter, and there wasn't a pool of blood, nothing except a young man bent in half and turning blue and slipping into unconsciousness.

Chapter Twenty-Seven

Oliver had a look on his face like he saw Megan standing before him as if she was on fire. Lester had made it back to town. By the time he heard on the police band that Chief Meghan Sheppard had apprehended the suspect, there was a crowd surrounding Nickolas Hodge's rental property. Most everyone who had access to a scanner heard Meghan on the radio calling for backup. She had to leave Hodge lying on the floor in the kitchen, covered in peanut butter and handcuffed to the stove handle before she ran to the police station and used the police band.

Kinguyakkii had an urgent care clinic but not a full hospital. There was a traveling doctor from time to time who came to town a few times a year. There was a woman named Jackie Qatalíña who worked full-time at the clinic. A physician assistant, she was the medical professional in town and arrived on scene twenty minutes after Meghan made the call.

Eric and Linda Kennedy arrived in the ice cream van. Even Duane Warren and Shelley Bass were there to watch as the chief of police, the physician assistant, and the coroner came out of the house, collectively shaking their heads.

"Anaphylaxis affects about 200,000 people in the United States. He doesn't have an epinephrine autoinjector," Jackie said with a shrug. "A man can't live that long and not know he had a severe peanut allergy." She tilted Meghan's head up with a gentle push with her knuckle under Meghan's chin. Examining the bruises left by Nickolas' grip, she continued to talk. "We don't have Nickolas on file at the clinic for any food allergies. Something that life-

152

threatening, I usually keep a close eye on." She gave Meghan a straight look. "You're lucky."

Eric stood back with Linda at his side. When Meghan saw him, he shook his head at her. "I'll take him if I can get some help."

"We need to get pictures, and I have to write up a report," Meghan said, retaking charge.

"How about you let your officers handle that," Calvin said. He slipped through the crowd and handed the digital camera to Oliver.

Grinning, Oliver took the camera and went into the house. Lester followed him.

"How are you doing?" Calvin asked. "If I knew you were going to tackle a suspected murderer alone, I would have come to help."

"I know, that's okay," Meghan said. She wasn't going to tell him that she'd gone to his trailer for help. The fact that Meghan had collected his fingerprints and briefly considered he was the killer was something she'd never share with him or anyone else. Meghan glanced to Duane. He was busy on the phone with someone, too caught up in the conversation to make eye contact with Meghan. It was a little after eleven on Thursday night, six days after Nickolas Hodge murdered Nancy McCormick, everyone was accounted for, and Meghan could with good conscious, officially close the case.

***

Once the adrenalin wore off, once the village settled, people went home, and had enough gossip to fuel months of anecdotes; Meghan followed Eric to the cold storage at the Ammattauq Native Trader Store. Lester and Oliver helped move Nickolas' body into the

153

cooler, put it on the floor beside the steel table where Nancy lay still wrapped in the house bedding.

"Eric, can you get Nickolas' pants off for me?" she asked casually.

Lester and Oliver gave her simultaneous looks that suggested she'd asked for something that was beyond her capacity as a police chief.

Eric obliged her, moving the wrap they used to carry Hodge's body into the cool so he could pull at the button and zipper. Her officers hung back by the cooler door watching in mute fascination.

"Is there a bruise on Nickolas' left thigh?"

"Um, yeah, looks like abrasion and a small hematoma on his upper thigh."

"Would you say that wound is consistent with someone running into a chair?" She huffed, feeling the burning in her veins from the dissolve of adrenalin. "Like maybe if a chair hit him."

"I couldn't say that conclusively."

"Well, it's good enough for me." Meghan needed to have confidence that the person who broke into the police department that night was Hodge, and not someone else tampering with evidence.

Oliver and Lester were chatting, standing at the cooler entrance. Meghan stood inside with Eric. She stared at Nancy's body.

"Let me get you, gentlemen, some salmon jerky." Eric moved out of the cool with Oliver and Lester in tow, leaving Meghan alone.

"I'm sorry this happened to you," Meghan said to Nancy. "I know it might not matter to you anymore, but I want you to know that we caught him. He can't do anything to anyone ever again."

Nancy lay peacefully on the steel table. Meghan wanted to believe that some part of the girl lingered, that she had been waiting to move on. Now that it was over, she could go and not be burdened by this life any longer.

"I wish I got to know you. You had a lot of friends here. People loved you." Reaching out, Meghan lightly tapped the wrapped foot on Nancy's corpse. "Goodnight, Nancy."

She left the cooler without looking or acknowledging the body of Nickolas Hodge and closed the door.

"My husband speaks highly of you," Linda Kennedy said when Meghan joined the small group on the main floor. Eric offered Meghan a homemade salmon jerky; it had been marinated in teriyaki sauce. It was delicious.

"Eric tells me you're the go-to person if I ever need a translator."

Linda smiled. "Maybe if you stick around long enough, you'll pick up more than you realize and won't need a translator."

"I think that's a great idea."

"What are we going to do with Hodge's body?" Oliver asked with a mouthful of jerky.

"I'll contact the troopers in the morning. I still have to write my report and submit it. My guess is they'll want to take his body to Anchorage for an autopsy."

155

"It's weird, isn't it?" Linda said. "Why would a guy that allergic to peanut butter have it in his house?"

"Maybe he didn't know. Maybe he didn't care."

"Maybe someone knew he had an allergy and put the peanut butter in his pantry."

The rest of the group went quiet, watching Oliver after he made the observation. It was a mystery, and while it was intriguing, Meghan had had enough for the day and wanted to go home and sleep.

"You want me to take the night shift?" Lester asked.

Meghan headed for the exit. "You two work that out between yourselves. I need to get a shower. I have peanut butter in my hair still. I'll see you both tomorrow. The three of us are going to close this murder case together. I want all our names on the docket." She looked back at her officers and her new friends. "I want to thank you guys for everything you've done."

"The town owes its gratitude to you, Meghan," Eric said. He put his arm around his wife and pulled her close.

Meghan wasn't big on kudos and waved "goodbye" while stepping outside.

"Need a lift?" Calvin asked, sitting in behind the wheel of the small green Ford Focus.

"How long you been waiting out here?"

"As long as it takes," he answered with a smile.

"I only live right over there." She pointed across the barren field. A few fifty-five gallon drums, a stack of wooden pallets, and a clump of dead fireweeds, that's all Meghan had to cross to get back to the house and end her day.

"I could walk you home."

She gave him a light smile, pushing coppery hair behind her ear. "I think I want to walk alone, clear my head."

He nodded. "I understand."

"It has nothing to do with you," she said quickly.

"You don't have to explain, Meghan, or make excuses. I'm not disappointed or angry. You'll be around. I'm not going anywhere." The engine revved and rattled when Calvin stepped on the accelerator. "I'll be seeing you." He drove away, turned the corner. Meghan made a mental note; the next time she saw Calvin she'd warn him about having a brake light out.

Chapter Twenty-Eight

By Friday afternoon Meghan had finished proofed and printed three copies of the incident report and the deposition for the murder investigation. She gave Lester and Oliver their copies and kept one for the main file. She emailed the final reports to Detective Anderson at the Alaska State Troopers office in Anchorage. There was a gentleman from the town who was quietly replacing the metal frame for the door to her office. Meghan didn't have to ask, didn't have to argue with Duane. Somehow, there was enough in the budget for a replacement door to her office.

She waited until after the man installed the new doorframe, patched the chipped drywall around the frame, and left before Meghan closed up the police station and made sure the doors were locked. She had three missed phone calls. No one left a voicemail, and two of the calls were numbers she didn't recognize, one was labeled 'private.' Meghan knew police officers using personal cell phones for communication paid the extra few dollars a month for the blocked number identification.

One of the numbers was listed 'mayor' on her contacts. She returned the call after she got home. Meghan was ready to settle down for the night but dressed in casual wear that made it easy if she had to run out the door again for emergencies.

"Meghan, thanks for returning my call," Duane said casually, "Even so late."

"No problem, what's up?" The man was informal, not quite relaxed, and the dig about it being late, it was barely after six in the evening, likely meant Meghan was supposed to call during regular business hours.

"I wanted you to make arrangements before we left so your officers can handle business while you're gone."

"Before I left?" she repeated.

"We're taking a trip into Anchorage tomorrow. The Borough Council is convening an emergency meeting, and they want you and I to attend."

A trip to Anchorage, she thought. They have money in the budget to fly the mayor and the police chief to Anchorage on a charter plane, but they can't afford toner cartridges, extra paper, express mail, plane tickets? No problem. She wasn't going to question it. Meghan knew better than ask the mayor about town business. Now she was inside the administrative circle, that place where the finer points of budgets and administration used to be left to someone else. It was never a good sign to have an emergency meeting, which usually meant someone was in trouble.

"What time are we leaving tomorrow?"

"Be at the airfield at eight-thirty."

"See you then." Meghan was fairly certain Duane ended the call before she finished her words.

Slipping on the bunny boots, oversized coat, ski cap, and gloves, Meghan left the house and walked up Bison Street to the small two-story house where Cheryl and Brian lived. Meghan kicked the mud off her boots before she knocked on the door.

The heavy footfalls inside told Meghan Brian was about to open the door. She presented a smile for him when the front door swung wide.

"Hey Chief," he said somberly, "Come in."

Kicking off the boots inside the door, Meghan followed Brian to where Cheryl sat with her feet tucked under her on the couch. The house had a stale cigarette smell that permeated everything.

"So, I have to leave tomorrow for Anchorage, police business. I wanted to stop in and see how you two were holding up." She let the words hang between Brian and Cheryl. They were quiet as if she'd interrupted a meaningful conversation. Meghan wasn't involved in the dialogue between the couple, and as long as it was a conversation and not a domestic dispute, it was none of her business. "Eric is able to hold Nancy for a little while. You can make arrangements with him when it comes time to take her." It was difficult to talk about because Meghan wanted to keep Nancy a person instead of a thing when it came to what to do next with her.

"We were talking about having her cremated." Cheryl got so far with her words before they stopped. It had been a week, grieving sometimes took years, it sometimes drove people apart.

"We're looking at taking out a small loan to cover the expenses. If it doesn't work out, we can wait until the ground thaws more and bury her here."

"Nancy would have liked staying here." Cheryl dabbed at her eyes with a tissue. "She always came home again."

Meghan nodded.

"We'll talk to Eric," Brian added. He looked hurt, not angry. "Maybe there's something we can work out."

"For what it's worth, I'm sorry."

160

"You have nothing to be sorry about, Meghan." Cheryl got off the couch and approached her. She wrapped her arms around Meghan and squeezed. "Thank you for everything. It felt like no one cared. You kept going."

"Sometimes when you don't see something doesn't mean there aren't things going on. You both had a lot on your plate. I was doing my job."

"You need to get a smaller parka," Cheryl mused.

"I like this coat. It was in the back of the Suburban when I got here. I washed it, and I know it's big, but I think it suits me." She held out her arms when Cheryl stepped back. "Keeps me warm."

"Well, in another month you won't need that heavy thing." Brian went to the kitchen counter to pick up a pack of cigarettes; Meghan used that as a cue to leave. "If you need anything you know you can call me." She went back to the door and slipped her feet into the boots.

"Thank you again, Meghan."

She nodded. It was never easy dealing with the death of a loved one. It was impossible to say anything that didn't sound glib. Sometimes a nod worked better than words.

"I'm not sure how long I'll be gone. Call the station if you need something if you can't get a hold of me."

Back outside, the ice fog had finally lifted earlier in the day. Above her, in the nautical twilight kept the clear sky lit with an azure tint only letting the brightest of the stars in the northern sky to flicker overhead.

161

Meghan took a deep breath, pulling in as much of the chilly arctic air as her lungs would hold. Things were changing. She'd put herself in danger apprehending a person who was suspect in a major violent crime. Meghan made a mistake, and she got lucky. The community expected her to keep them safe. She lived in a world that is a little different than anywhere else in the United States. Nothing should be taken for granted.

The walk home gave her time to reflect, on the job, her life, and the choices she made to get to where she was at that moment. Retiring as an FBI Agent to take over as Chief of Police in Kinguyakkii, four thousand miles from where she grew up, Meghan felt in that moment she hadn't run away from anything, she was right where she was supposed to be, and it felt good.

Chapter Twenty-Nine

The central seat of government in Alaska is Juneau. An isolated, landlocked community that sat on the corner of the last temperate rainforest in the United States; surrounded by overgrown broadleaf forests and coniferous trees, it was a vacation destination for millions of people every year traveling on cruise ships. Picturesque, the state capital left indelible impressions on anyone who came to Alaska as a visitor but didn't live there.

Anchorage, Alaska, was a city like many cities in the northwest United States. Weather was a little more predictable than most of the outlining towns along with the Alaska Highway system. The largest city in the state, most patronage was done in the Cook Inlet city, considered the gateway to mountain ranges that included Talkeetna, Chugach, and Kenai.

Flying low over the city, the charter plane was snug and loud. They were on what essentially was an air taxi service. The price per hour for the particular flight out of Kinguyakkii to Anchorage, landing at the small airport of Merrill Field, was more than two months' salary for Meghan and while she wanted to enjoy the flight, see the vast mountain ranges and wilderness terrain, it was hard to look down when part of the wing had duct tape on it, and a piece of it had feathered and flapped in the high winds like a dog ear hanging out a car window.

Instead, Meghan drew up her legs, pressed her shoulder against the fuselage of the Cessna 180 while Duane sat in the copilot seat up front and chatted with their pilot. She had to listen to the sputtering engine and the whining through the aluminum membrane of the aircraft.

In the back of the plane was the body of Nickolas Hodge, secured in a tarp with ropes. It wasn't pretty, but it was efficient. There was supposed to be an ambulance crew waiting for the charter plane when they landed. It was something the Borough Council worked out with the medical examiner's office in Anchorage. Eric had sent the preliminary cause of death along with the physician assistant's signature for corroboration. Someone was paying the bill for transporting the corpse of a killer, but the victim remained in cold storage at a trading store. Somehow, that didn't seem fair to Meghan.

When they landed at Merrill Field off Fifth Avenue two miles from downtown Anchorage, it was after five in the evening and whatever Duane had planned he wasn't sharing with Meghan.

"The Borough booked us rooms at the hotel on Third Avenue. It's nice," Duane said, handing Meghan her travel bag. He was the kind of guy who wanted to be in charge of everything, including things that were none of his business. He was a jerk, plain and simple. "We'll catch a ride to the hotel together." He grinned like a hero. "My treat," he added. It wasn't; Duane would get a receipt from the taxi driver and turn it in with the monthly expense report to get reimbursed.

***

Anchorage was the first stop Meghan had when she took the job as police chief. It had been a few years since she returned. Everything Meghan owned was either in Kinguyakkii or back home in Syracuse, New York, including a daughter. Brittany was independent at fifteen. When Meghan split up with her ex-husband, Meghan allowed Brittany to choose to stay in New York or to follow her mother on an adventure into the Alaska wilderness. The internet

164

was slow, and cell phone signals were spotty, she'd have to change schools and leave friends behind.

It was a tough decision allowing her to stay with her father. A man who was a good dad but a terrible husband, whatever differences Meghan had with the man, she wasn't malicious and wasn't going to use Brittany to get back at her father. They sometimes emailed, when Brittany found time to do it.

Meghan kept up with her daughter's grades through the integrated services the school provided. She was abreast of all Brittany's grades, including progress reports. They talked on the phone at least once a week, and her daughter wanted to show Meghan how to use social media to keep up-to-date on all the trending topics. Meghan knew how to use social media; she chose to keep out of the spotlight.

"Hey Mom," Brittany said when Meghan called after she arrived at the hotel. Alaska had its own time zone, four hours behind New York. It was after ten in New York, but on Saturday nights, Brittany was up late, usually with her friends. It was something that worried Meghan, but she knew her ex-husband as much as a lousy human being as he was, he was actively involved in his daughter's life, and wouldn't let her out past a curfew or hang out with people he didn't know.

Her voice was musical to Meghan. There is nothing like the connection between mother and daughter, and even if she were a million miles away, those two little words would carry her.

"Sorry I didn't call last Saturday," Meghan said.

"That's okay; me and Dad went to the movies."

"That's good. What are you doing now? It's loud over there."

"I'm at a friend's house. We're hanging out."

"A boy?" Meghan wanted to be there for her daughter, no matter how far away, mothers and daughters show be able to talk about things that mattered to both of them. Unfortunately, either Brittany made sure she was never available for a full conversation with her mother, or her life was so full of other things, Meghan wasn't a big part of anymore. Before she sunk into a depression that sapped her mental strength, something that Brittany seemed to pick up on, she made a joke.

"No, but we have male strippers coming over later." She laughed, and her girlfriend nearby laughed loud enough for Meghan to hear through the phone. "What have you been doing? I bet it's boring as shit over there."

"Brittany, please don't cuss." She sighed. It was a show, Brittany's swearing while talking with her mother was meant to impress a friend. It was the kind of thing Meghan did with her mother. "It's been pretty boring. Same old thing," she said, lying across the bed, staring at the ceiling in the hotel suite. If only her daughter knew what kind of a week she had, it might actually impress her. "So, we all set for you coming to see me when school lets out?"

"Yeah, but do I need to bring like a snowsuit or mittens and snow boots?"

"It's not like that." Brittany had passed on visiting her mother last year. The flight across the country as an unaccompanied minor bothered the girl too much. She was more self-determining now, freer to explore her surroundings. She was still considered a minor with the airlines, but Meghan had a few friends with the air marshals and would make Brittany's trip memorable. "You'll be able to wear fall gear around. It gets up to 60 or 70°F in the summer. The sun's always up. Kids are out all night."

Summer was busy; more people came to town from the villages. It wasn't always lovely people that showed up to town. While she'd be active, there was still time for her daughter. That is if Meghan kept her job after the meeting with the emergency council tomorrow.

There was more noise on Brittany's end. People were talking close to her ear. Someone said, "Hurry up," and Meghan knew what came next.

"I got to get going, Mom."

"I know. Enjoy your Saturday night. I'm watching your progress reports. You are going to get that social studies grade up before the school year ends." It wasn't a question, it was necessary.

"I will. It's so boring."

"I don't see how a girl in today's technology-dependent world doesn't get easy A's in social studies."

Brittany growled in frustration. "Okay, Mom. I got to go."

"I know. I love you."

"I love you back. Bye." The call ended.

Brittany went back to her busy teenage life, and Meghan made herself comfortable, flipping channels, taking advantage of a quiet night. She scooted under the covers and forgot about everything, left behind a crazy moment in her life that could have left Brittany without a mother.

It was the second time in Meghan's life she'd faced an untimely death. She wasn't carrying a gun, but the job turned out to be just as dangerous.

Chapter Thirty

There were five visible North Slope Borough Council members at the large table in an upstairs meeting room at one of the offices off C Street after nine in the morning on Sunday. Duane collected Meghan a half hour before the scheduled meeting. They checked out of the hotel and were expected to fly back to Kinguyakkii by three in the afternoon.

"Thank you for coming, Chief Sheppard." They didn't bother introducing themselves. Meghan recognized one of the women who were on the video conference call when she first was hired for the job but forgot names since most of the members didn't live in Kinguyakkii. They looked at her as if she had a choice to come to the meeting.

There were a few different cameras on the table. There was a flat screen monitor on the wall behind the inquisition group facing Meghan, more board members sitting in on the meeting from the comfort of their homes, split into four different views from various locations, they leisurely sipped coffee or smoked cigarettes while watching Meghan.

"You've had a busy week. We've been kept up-to-date on what's been going on in your little corner of the world." The speaker was a woman who looked to be in her fifties. She was heavy-set with bifocals. There were copies of emails in front of her. Meghan suspected while she was investigating Nancy's death, Duane was busy keeping tabs on her. Likely, that was one of the reasons he wanted access to her office.

Duane shifted in the seat he took at the beginning of the meeting. He joined the other board members facing Meghan while she sat alone opposite them.

"We all appreciate everything you do for us. This is an informal meeting. If it involved more than the administration, finance, and the mayor's office, we would have convened a regular meeting. I hope you don't mind."

Meghan smiled, rolling her hair behind her ear. "You're being so nice to me. I feel like if you have some bad news, you should tell me, like ripping off a band-aid."

The council members exchanged glances. "You're not in any trouble, Chief Sheppard. This isn't a reprimand." The woman glared at Duane as if he'd not made it clear to her why they had a meeting. "Mayor Warren should have explained to you that we wanted to address some ongoing budget issues within the Kinguyakkii Police Department." She shuffled through the documents in front of her until she found a copy of the receipt from the FBI center in Quantico. Meghan recognized the letterhead. "When Duane sent this to me, I got a case of sticker shock. But when we discussed it, we realized that your department has been operating in a vacuum for more than a few years. We haven't had someone in your position that frankly, many of us took seriously."

Another council member spoke up immediately. "Let's not hash out the past in front of the current police chief, okay Valerie?"

Valerie went on speaking to Meghan as if it was just the two of them in the considerable space. "We're looking at increasing your expenditure budget, Chief Sheppard. We need something that will work for all of us. You might not think that this kind of expense is extraordinary, but our mayor has pulled the city out of significant red since he's taken office. It might seem like micromanaging, and while I admit from

170

experience, Duane can be a little pushy at times." She looked from Meghan and smiled at Duane before continuing. "Sometimes, in life, we run into people who we need to play our foils to make the balance work properly." She shook her head. "Before you go on another spending spree, try to talk to Duane first. If you feel like you're hitting a wall, you can always call me."

She folded her hands together on the stack of recipes and gave Meghan all her attention. "Tell us, Chief Sheppard, what would make your work easier. What can we do today to start making plans to incorporate in the near future?"

While she suspected most people would have immediately asked for a raise, Meghan felt she received the right amount of money for the job she did. It was a good income with great potential for retirement. Now Meghan knew she didn't have to look for other employment, that she was staying where she was, she could settle in, maybe finish unpacking those few extra boxes stacked in the corner of the house.

"I'd like another full-time officer. Maybe a reserve officer or a few who can give my people some better hours, so no one is working seven days, twelve-hour shifts. It might even cut back on the overtime we put in every week."

Valerie smiled. "I like the sound of that. You've been working for a larger organization for most of your career. Can I assume this is the first time you've had to work with the budget end of things?"

Meghan only nodded. Bureaucracy wasn't something she wanted to learn or stay in for any length of time. She loved the thrill of the chase, the minutiae of solving the case.

"I'd like to see if the town can help with Nancy McCormick's body? Her sister and brother-in-law run the restaurant and—"

"Yes, the Midnight Sun Café," Valerie said. She nodded slowly. "I always go there when I visit. We'll make an arrangement with the family to take care of a daughter of Kinguyakkii."

Everything went better than expected, and Meghan sat back in the chair, pleasantly surprised and satisfied with the overall meeting.

"Is there anything else we can do for you, Chief Sheppard?" This time it was one of the mute members who watched from the video monitor. She suspected it was another subtle jab at her asking for a raise.

"No, I think we're all set." Then she thought quickly. "I'd like the department to have a digital camera. We need something to use in case we have something else happen. Sometimes the cameras on our phones just don't cut it."

"Well, find what you need on the internet. Send me the link. I'll make sure you get that or something comparable."

"Thank you."

"We're all set here." Three out of the four members watching the meeting from their homes switched off. Valerie gathered the rest of her paperwork, slipped it into a manila folder, and stood up. Meghan stood, pushed in the chair on the plush carpet of the boardroom, and waited.

"Chief Sheppard, can I see you a moment?" Valerie said.

Meghan walked around the large oak table, following the woman down a hallway to the side of the

172

meeting area. The other board members present went in a different direction, including Duane.

Valerie slipped through a door at the end of the long hallway, and Meghan reached the doorway when Valerie placed the file folder on an expansive desk. Valarie turned to face Meghan, smiling.

"So, working with Duane is not too easy, is it?"

Rather than agree, to admit the truth, Meghan knew better than feed into opening a door that was impossible to close again.

"All I can say is to work around him as best you can. I've known Duane for a long time. He can be a bit of an asshole, but I can't think of anyone else who cares for that town as much as he does."

"I feel like there's another agenda with him sometimes."

"It's no secret that he wanted someone else in your place. After the fiasco with the corruption charges against the former chief, we have to play it close to the chest. Don't take this the wrong way, or think we're insensitive, but you're an outsider, and that's exactly what that town needs in a chief." Valerie handed Meghan a business card. It was thick, embossed, and had all her private information on it. "Call me, day or night, if you need something."

She folded her arms, watching Meghan tuck the card into a pocket. "I feel like you thought this meeting was going in a different direction as we ambushed you."

"That's kind of how it felt, yes."

"You had limited resources; you solved a murder investigation by yourself in less than a week. Why in the world would you think you were in trouble?"

"Well, I wasn't alone, I had help, Lester and Oliver both did great jobs. It would be nice if we had a little more issued for personal safety than pepper spray."

"That's a little outside my field, Chief Sheppard. It's something the entire Council has to weigh in on, and I don't see anything changing soon. The Alaska State Troopers have jurisdiction on what we can and can't issue our officers. There's talk about further incorporating the city. Once it reaches a certain capacity, we have no choice than build jails, hire more officers, and issue firearms. Right now, the best you can get is another cop and more pepper spray."

"How about a taser?" Meghan asked. It wasn't too far away from pepper spray and still nonlethal.

Valerie laughed. "For someone who doesn't want much, your list might be longer than you realize. How about I'll see what I can do. Sometimes it doesn't hurt to ask."

Chapter Thirty-One

While they didn't talk much, Duane and Meghan shared a taxi back to Merrill Field to wait until their charter flight was ready to leave. Meghan sat inside the hanger, watching the crew load the small plane with supplies. Any trip to and from villages were perfect conduits to transport any variety of supplies.

Meghan sipped on cold coffee from a paper cup while she scanned digital cameras using the internet on her smartphone.

An unmarked car pulled up to the airstrip, rolling by the small Cessna 180 that was getting ready to take off. Merrill Field was a general aviation public-use small airport. Small independent flights used the airfield because it had easier access than the international airport where most of the tourists used when flying in and out of Anchorage, Alaska.

The airstrip was designated for life-flights because it was a half mile from the nearest hospital. The troopers used the airfield when they had unregistered flight plans that took them into the bush when they were hunting poachers or bootleggers.

When a cop rolled up on the tarmac, no one took notice of the vehicle. Since they had the credentials to get through security, none of the pilots or passengers cared where they were headed, as long as the cops weren't coming for the pilot or guests.

"You Sheppard?" the man asked from inside the Dodge Charger, passenger window down, head tipped to look at her from the other side of mirrored sunglasses. The guy couldn't pretend to be anything else except a cop. The car was sleek, new, and shiny black. The interior had been overhauled and fitted with a see-through partition that separated the driver from the rear passengers in case the officer transported dangerous suspects.

"Who wants to know?" she asked. If he wanted to play cartoon cop, Meghan would oblige him with her version of comic book cliché dialogue.

The sunglasses shifted, pushed down the bridge of his nose with a finger so he could look at her without the lenses. "Are you for real?" he asked.

She smiled and said, "I should ask the same of you."

She pulled herself from the lounge chair inside the hanger. It was mildly entertaining watching the pilot and the cargo handlers trying to pack the plane full of supplies headed for the village. Meghan tried to ignore the weight they managed to get on the flight because she had to fly across miles of jagged mountain peaks on her way back to the village.

Meghan put the coffee on the table near the hanger door and wandered out to the black Charger. She leaned over and got a better look at the driver. He was cop through and through. Overweight, overdressed in a two-piece suit and broke the golden rule about wearing a blazer while driving. Clearly, no one taught this man to hang the jacket when he was behind the wheel. His stomach touched the steering wheel as he motioned for her to climb in.

"Am I going to miss my flight if I get in the car?" She glanced to Duane, who sat by himself deeper inside the hanger. He'd been on the business laptop and his phone most of the afternoon. If they were supposed to call a truce, it still hadn't happened, and Meghan didn't think Duane was the kind of man to admit he was a little over the top when it came to managing the town or keeping all the cards to himself.

She didn't wait for the detective to give her any real answer before opening the passenger door and climbing inside. The detective was heavy on the accelerator, pulling away from the hanger, swinging the car around on the tarmac and driving back toward the gate.

He got as far as the security gate before pulling over.

Once the car was in park, the detective extended his hand toward Meghan. "Chief Meghan Sheppard."

Meghan shook his hand. "That's funny; that's my name too," she said, and added, "Detective Gregory Anderson."

"Just Greg is fine."

"Meghan." His beefy hand was steady and moist. Meghan absently wiped her hand on her thigh. "What can I do for you, Detective?"

"You come to town and don't stop in to say hello?"

"I didn't know you wanted to see me," she admitted. "I don't get a lot of extra information from the town if you happened to contact someone."

"I got a call from the ME about the body coming into town. A suspect in a murder investigation was dead, and you know how it is, we have to investigate the cops in case you killed the killer."

She shook her head. "That wasn't me. He had an allergic reaction. That was all him, or genetics."

There was a manila file on the dashboard that Detective Anderson reached for and shoved toward Meghan. "That's our side of your investigation. You officially solved Nancy McCormick's murder. That was serious police work."

Meghan looked through the file. There was more information about Nickolas Hodge. She began to scan the first page, but Anderson talked over her, concentrating on the paperwork.

"We matched his fingerprints to an unsolved case in Arizona. Hodge wasn't even on the radar down there."

"Was it in Mesa or Phoenix?" she asked.

"How did you know about Mesa?" Anderson gave her a look that suggested she knew more than he did. "There was a twenty-three-year-old college student who waitressed tables at a diner in Mesa. Five years ago, Hodge lived in Mesa before he moved to Phoenix. He came up to Alaska three years ago after he got a job with a real estate outfit in Wasilla managing apartment complexes. From there he found a job in your town doing the same thing."

Meghan nodded. She wasn't much for profiling, never got the specialized training; she used the casework when it was available from other agents. Not every killer got a workup, but Hodge seemed to follow a pattern that she wouldn't have noticed last week.

"So, this waitress," she asked. "Was she strangled in her apartment?"

"She was," Anderson said with a slow nod. "They never matched a suspect to the crime because they were looking for a Latino man who was seen near the apartment building the night of the girl's murder. Hodge wasn't on file, and the sheriff's department was too busy being colorblind to see straight." It was a dig at the racial tension that still went on in the Border States.

"Was he ever in the military?" she asked.

"Wow, I think you should come work for us," Anderson said. "Did you see that in the file already?"

"No, he had army issue gloves; at least that's what they looked like. He left one glove in the bedroom. I know I sent you pictures of it."

"Yeah, I remember. He washed out of boot camp, something to do with an unhealthy mental status. They let him keep the basic issue garb."

"Killing Nancy wasn't intentional. Not that I saw. I think something was going on in Hodge that he hadn't quite worked out yet. It doesn't surprise me; it was the second time for him." She stared out the windshield. There was a low-flying prop plane on approach. It was a clear evening; the sun was still hovering above the Tordrillo Mountains to the northwest of the Anchorage Bowl. Slight wind, the plane floated down to the tarmac and landed with little effort. "If this guy got away with it, he would have made it a habit."

"So, what's the deal? Peanut butter?" Anderson said frowning. "That's one story for the books."

"Isn't that like flirting with disaster? I don't know what happens inside a guy's head, but to have something that serious to his health makes me wonder if Hodge even knew it was in the cupboard."

Anderson belly laughed. "That's one for the books for sure. To think that maybe someone knew he was deathly allergic and just put it in the house."

"I'm thinking the peanut butter was already in the pantry when Hodge got to the house. I can tell you that I wasn't looking when I grabbed the jar and hit him with it. It was blind luck. He was choking me

179

out, and my hand wrapped around the jar." She shook her head. "I think the house belongs to Blue Sky Realty. It was one of Hodge's perks for dealing with the apartments in town. A prior tenant probably left it in the pantry, and he never knew it was there. I'm not going to read into it."

Anderson was interested in her tale, but Meghan didn't want to deal with the emotions that came with thinking about dying at the hands of a wannabe serial killer. She shook her head, shook out the dark figure that had its hands wrapped around her throat before she happened to find the right tool to take him out.

"Are they going to let you have a gun now?" Anderson was savvy enough to know when to change the subject.

"That's not going to happen. I don't know if you have any pull with the troopers in charge of the Village Public Safety Program, but maybe you can get them to issue me a taser at least."

"That's a good idea. Unfortunately, that's not my department, and I don't know what kind of politics is involved with running that program."

"Me either."

They were quiet for a minute. Meghan saw by the clock on the dashboard. They had about fifteen minutes before she had to board the Cessna 180 back to Kinguyakkii.

"You know I was serious about you coming to work with us. You could earn your detective badge in a few years. Your experience goes a long way."

"It's tempting, but I kind of like what I do."

"You probably have a lot fewer headaches than we do. You don't have someone breathing down your neck wondering if keeping you on the payroll is worth it."

"Oh, I have one of those, and he's standing right over there." Meghan pointed to Duane who wandered out of the hanger and scanned the area for Meghan. She knew he'd get on that plane and leave with or without her.

Detective Anderson put the car in drive and rolled ahead along the edge of the runaway. With a departure flight scheduled it was unlikely that the detective's car was in the way of oncoming air traffic. He pulled up to the hanger, and Meghan got out of the vehicle. She reached back through the open window and shook Anderson's hand again.

"Don't be a stranger, Sheppard."

"You should come up and see us."

Anderson laughed. "I doubt you'll have any use for a violent crimes detective in your end of the woods any time soon. It's been over twenty years since your last homicide."

"Fifteen years actually," Meghan corrected. "I don't suppose you can get me a copy of that cold case, can you?"

"Are you looking to solve that too while you're chief of police out there?"

She shrugged. "It doesn't hurt to take a look at the file, have it on hand in case something comes up."

"I'll see what I can do, Sheppard."

"Stay safe, Greg."

"You too Meghan," he said and revved the engine swinging the Charger around to head back

181

through the security gate. Boys and their toys never end.

The flight back from Anchorage to Kinguyakkii was bumpy. It was well after nine-thirty before the plane touched down. Meghan had the passenger seats to herself and managed to take a nap until the turbulence shook her awake again.

Shelley Bass was waiting at the airport for Duane. He collected his travel bag as Meghan grabbed her small suitcase. She was ready to call Oliver or Lester, whoever was on duty to come to pick her up at the airport when Duane spoke up.

"Need a lift, Chief?" he asked. They were halfway across the tarmac when he called to her.

Meghan caught up to them without words and climbed into the back seat beside the cardboard file boxes Shelley had on the rear seat. Duane didn't say anything before Shelley dropped her off at the house on Bison Street.

"Thank you," she said, climbing out of the car.

Shelley smiled. "Bye."

"See you Monday," Duane said, and as the car pulled away, Meghan saw in the streetlight, Duane reached over and put his hand on the driver's seat.

She wasn't one to pry, to read into innocent gestures. Shelley wore a wedding ring. Duane was an authority figure and Shelley's immediate supervisor. Whatever went on between them, as long as they weren't breaking the law, had nothing to do with Meghan.

She unlocked the front door to the house, kicked off her boots, and shed the jacket. She'd left the bunny boots and oversized parka in Kinguyakkii. It was night and day when it came to the weather between the two cities. She had other gear that wasn't so heavy, and it felt odd not to wear a coat that was heavy and warm and too big for her.

Meghan made it as far as the couch. Put down her head, pulled her knees up to her chest, and pulled the blanket that hung over the back of the sofa. She slept there throughout the better part of Sunday.

Chapter Thirty-Two

Monday arrived without surprises. Oliver had a smile on his face, sitting at the front counter when Meghan arrived promptly at eight. The Chevy Suburban complained when she tried starting it, gurgling and sputtering from the house to the police department.

Next door Shelley's car parked parallel to town hall, telling Meghan that the office administrator or the mayor, or both were already at their respective workplaces. The clear sky from overnight continued into the morning, and sunrise was twelve minutes earlier than Sunday. In another two months, dawn would be hours earlier, creep along with the distant mountain ranges and foothills, encircling the small town nestled at the end of a spit on the peninsula that poked out into Kinguyakkii Sound. By midsummer sunset would be a distant memory and something to look forward to until the ginger orb left the sky for the other side of the planet, leaving the Arctic in the dark for the months of winter. Life in Alaska was always a little different, and that was something Meghan liked about it.

"Good morning, Boss." Oliver had made a fresh pot of coffee. The aroma greeted Meghan along with his pleasant smile.

The local AM radio station was on. The resident DJ, White Noise Wayne, was reading the local weather report for inland and at sea. He and Dead-Air Dave had a morning talk show that mostly covered television shows and upcoming local events. When Meghan heard Nancy McCormick mentioned, she stopped moving around to listen.

184

White-Noise Wayne continued, "As you all probably know, our wonderful waitress from Midnight Sun Café was found dead in her apartment last Saturday night. Our very own Kinguyakkii Police Chief, Meghan Sheppard apprehended the suspect single-handedly."

"That's not true," she interjected without the DJ's knowledge.

"We are grateful for our Kinguyakkii Police and all the hard work they do there. Donations for Nancy's family can be made at Midnight Sun Café, show your support, give something back to the community."

"Thank you, Wayne," Dead-Air Dave added. They wanted to have a celebrity radio talk show like counterparts from lower-forty-eight radio stations. Since the AM broadcast was nonprofit, they could ramble and talk about anything they wanted. They took requests and programmed the overnight music to play nonstop without commercial interruption. That's when Meghan usually listened to the radio. Dead-Air Dave and White-Noise Wayne tried to be funny; mostly they skirted FCC violations by making innuendos instead of direct statements.

"What do you think about our police chief, Wayne?" Dead-Air Dave asked.

"I think she's doing a fine job. I've never met her personally but—"

"I have."

"Have what?"

"I've met her, personally. I mean, I saw her up close once. She was shopping at the store when I was there."

"Which store? Ammattauq Native Trader or Alaska Merchandise? And can someone tell me why they call it Alaska Merchandise? I mean, we're in Alaska, we all know, that right?"

"Well, you can't call it Merchandise Store," Dave countered. "That's just silly."

"Not as silly as what they call it. It'd be different if the store were in California or Iowa, then you'd call it—"

"So, I met the chief," Dave interrupted the tangent with a segue.

"Oh, right. What'd you think?"

"She's nice. She seems tough, you know like she could kill you with a jar of peanut butter."

Meghan bristled. She veered toward the radio near the coffeemaker. Wayne and Dave continued with their banter. Word got out, someone; probably a lot of people were talking about the case. The bizarre accident was bound to take precedence over the fact that Nancy McCormick was a victim. Now Nickolas Hodge would be a local hot topic for a while. People would remember his name, mainly because it was death by peanut butter. Most people never remembered the names of victims, only the killers.

"She's a looker too," Dave said over the air, hundreds of people listening. Suddenly Meghan felt a flush of heat from embarrassment. "I mean she's older, you know, but she's really attract—"

"Morning, Oliver," she said after the radio was off.

Whatever the two men had to say about her to the rest of the town and the surrounding countryside, anywhere the AM signal reached, including across the

186

bay and into the Bering Sea, it wasn't anything Meghan wanted to hear. She took a breath, felt the hammering of her heart, and pretended that whatever was on the radio had nothing to do with her. There was a little part of Meghan that was flattered; another part of her felt the weight of her hips and the festering of the words 'she's older' that was going to haunt her for a long time.

She made her way through the little gate, gave an approving nod to the new doorframe. While the patchwork was visible, it needed a paint job. Then she put her key into the doorknob and sighed.

"What's wrong?" Oliver asked.

"He changed the lock again." Meghan shook her head, removed the old key from the key ring, and threw it in the trash by the coffee counter. She shed her coat, tossed it on the table, and fixed a cup of coffee.

What was it that Valerie called Duane? A foil? What was it she learned in college about the literary device? Duane was supposed to contrast her, provided she was some sort of hero or protagonist. She did happen to solve a murder within a few days. That must have something to do with her status. Of course, a lot of it was guesswork and pure dumb luck — particular aspects of solving the case she'd never freely admit. Duane, for whatever reason, rubbed Meghan the wrong way like sandpaper underwear. She had to put up with him and eventually find a balance.

There was the drop and scrape of something across the table. Meghan saw a split key ring with two keys on it. She followed the sudden appearance of the keys to Oliver still smiling at her like he kept pudding

187

in his pocket and wanted people to guess what he carried around with him.

"Mayor Warren dropped these off this morning. He's getting the outside locks changed too."

Meghan picked up the keys, looked at them suspiciously. Two keys usually came with replacement doorknob. Were these the only two keys for the office door or did he have one as well? She'd have to order another doorknob, identical to the new one and replace it when no one was around.

"Anything out of the ordinary happen while I was away?" she asked and tried one of the keys in the door lock.

"Lester had a shoplifter on Sunday. It was one of the Jones kids from Ptarmigan Way. Lester chased him on foot from the store."

"That's a long way from Alaska Merchandise Store. If he knew who the kid was, why'd he chase him?"

Oliver shrugged. "Wasn't anything else going on."

That was a good sign. Their little slice of the world was balanced again, quiet. She got into the office and hung up her coat on the hook by the door. Meghan sat down at her desk and felt as if she'd come home again.

There was an email from Jeff Ravenswaay, Andrea's son. The attachments were links to online servers. When the video files downloaded, she watched them, one after another. Out of eighteen people who walked by Andrea's apartment, the figure that hurried by, caught in a blur on the way out of the building using the side door, had the same shape and consistency as Nickolas Hodge. If the man had lived to stand trial, she'd have more than enough to convince a jury he was Nancy's killer.

Chapter Thirty-Three

Cheryl and Brian Snyder closed the Midnight Sun Café for the entire weekend following Meghan's return to town from Anchorage. Kinguyakkii Cemetery had very little organization when it came to plots. Sometimes during the summer months, when the ground softened enough for people to dig graves, families got together and took turns digging the hole. There were a few diggers in town, small backhoes that owners loaned out when people had money to rent for a few hours. The Snyders didn't need the backhoe, and when it came to digging the grave for Nancy, most of the town showed up to help.

Meghan stood with the family while Eric coordinated how to handle the remains because, of course, he was the city's undertaker. There didn't seem to be any end of the hats the man wore for Kinguyakkii.

It was a beautiful Saturday afternoon when Cheryl and Brian lay Nancy to rest. People respectfully added their condolences and Meghan got her share of handshakes. She wanted to make sure the townspeople knew it was Nancy's day, not hers.

Afterward, there was a gathering at the Cultural Civic Center on Second Avenue near the museum. It was the mayor's contribution to the burial of Nancy McCormick. While Meghan suspected the Borough Council had something to do with opening the door, paying for refreshments, Duane took all the credit and made sure that everyone who showed up shook hands with him, making the occasion all about Duane instead of Nancy.

"You look a little put out." The observation came from Calvin who dressed for the occasion, wearing a pressed blue shirt, flat black tie, and black blazer with black slacks. He looked great, smelled terrific.

Meghan sipped at the punch from the concessions table and tried avoiding his hazel eyes. Calvin had shaved the bristles from his face too, showing the lean, strong jawline.

"I'm not, really." Maybe her feelings about Duane taking over the banquet had soured her mood, more than just saying goodbye to a woman she barely knew. "I'm just thinking, is all," she said because it was safer than speaking her mind.

"Is it because Duane made this all about him and not about Nancy?" he asked.

Meghan smiled at him. There it was, handsome, observant, and giving her a look that suggested she was either overdressed or underdressed. Meghan dressed for a party. It was a social event, something that didn't happen very often. Other people in town looked at it the way she did.

Cheryl and Brian, whatever marital problems they had, looked satisfied with each other and were mingling and laughing with people. Alaskans thought it was better to celebrate a person's life than ruin a social event with sadness. Nancy, from what Meghan learned, had touched a lot of lives, mostly in useful ways. She always wore a bright smile when they visited the diner, and she gave everyone conversations and coffee.

Usually, the closest to social events in town happened when bingo went into overtime, or the volunteer fire department purchased extra fireworks for New Years. Fireworks on the Fourth of July weren't worth a damned in Kinguyakkii because fireworks in daylight don't cut it.

191

"You look really nice," he commented.

"Thank you, so do you."

Meghan let down her hair. The weather turned; a little less humidity meant she'd regained some natural wave back to her hair. She considered herself off-duty, so the one and the only dress she brought with her from New York was a semi-formal dress with a long skirt. It wasn't flashy but had a deep V-neck top, showing more of her neckline than Meghan remembered ever showing in Alaska. Under the fluorescent lights of the civic hall, her skin looked pasty white. She wore low heel boots that didn't show up under the skirt. Since it was impossible for anyone to know, Meghan had black leggings under the dress to keep her legs warm.

"I read your article in the *Northern Lights Sounder*," Meghan said conversationally.

"You did?" He sipped on a plastic cup of punch. "What did you think of it?"

Since it was a dry village, the non-alcoholic punch had a variety of ingredients, including ginger ale, apple, orange, and cranberry juices. It was thick and bitter, but at least it wasn't lethal.

There was an assortment of homemade dishes to pass — traditional Alaskan dishes mixed with store-bought treats. The buffet table was diverse, and parts of it had strange odors.

"I thought it was good. I wasn't too keen about seeing my face on the front page."

Calvin nodded without a retort. He gave her a look that suggested he had something to tell her but held back.

"Looks like Duane is about to make a speech." Calvin motioned behind Meghan where the mayor, his assistant, and the local DJs were huddled at the PA system where there had been a collection of contemporary and country music playing until Duane took over.

"Ladies and gentlemen," he said into the microphone. The PA system was owned by the radio station and on loan along with the volunteer DJs. Both Dead-Air Dave and White-Noise Wayne were looking across the gathering of people on the main floor, and Meghan saw them share looks, lean close and talk. She tried to ignore the fact they had made eye contact with her and were likely continuing a private conversation about Meghan that had started over the airwaves earlier in the week.

"I want to thank everyone for coming tonight, showing support to Cheryl and Brian Snyder while we celebrate Nancy McCormick's life with them. She was a daughter of Kinguyakkii and will be missed."

Meghan smiled at the comment because she'd heard the phrase somewhere before. While it was unintentional, when the mayor started his speech, she wandered closer to the riser at the south end of the gathering hall. When there were events at the civic center, the riser helped everyone see without having to peer around big shoulders.

Meghan got a little closer to the stage because most of the people in front of her were much taller, rounder than her. Calvin walked close behind her. Time to time, she felt his hand gently press against the small of her back, letting her know he was still close.

When she found an area among the crowd where she could see Duane, the DJs, and the rest of the stage, Meghan turned to look at Calvin. He'd slipped away from her, wandered to the far side of the hall, leaving her standing beside a local resident who paid more attention to her than Duane.

"I would like everyone to give a round of applause to Chief Meghan Sheppard," Duane continued. People responded with cheers and applause that made her very uncomfortable. "Chief Sheppard, could you come up here a moment."

"That's okay, Mayor!" she called from the crowd. "I'm fine right here." Meghan lifted a hand in acknowledgment.

"Please, Chief Sheppard," he asked. It sounded sincere. He joined in the clapping as she moved through the bodies and went to the stage.

Dead-Air Dave reached out, offering Meghan a hand to step up on the riser. She took his hand and smiled politely.

"Chief Sheppard, everyone," Duane said into the microphone, added clapping. The gathering was much bigger than Meghan first suspected. From the stage, it was easier to see most of the village showed up.

She had nothing to say, instead just lifted a palm again to the audience. Calvin came across the stage, carrying a large picture frame covered in a cloth. Duane backed away from the microphone. Meghan was surprised to see Calvin step up and address the audience.

"Ladies and gentlemen, a lot of you know me as the local reporter for the *Northern Lights Sounder*. I'm here tonight not only as a reporter for the paper but

194

as a person who received an extraordinary opportunity recently that I want to share with the rest of you."

Meghan stood between Dead-Air Dave and White-Noise Wayne. Both men squeezed close to her, invading her personal bubble. She tried to ignore their competitiveness and figure out what Calvin was up to with the speech, and why the hell they needed her on stage.

"It is a great honor when a struggling journalist gets an opportunity to reach the acclaim of national coverage. A lot of you may not think it's a big thing, but I can tell you from personal experience that it's not only a good thing for me, but for the *Northern Lights Sounder*. I had an opportunity to reach across the United States when one of my articles was published with the *Associated Press*. Because of the fine police work from Kinguyakkii's very own Chief Meghan Sheppard, I've gotten the opportunity once again to have an article published."

Duane and Calvin handled the picture frame. Calvin pulled the cloth from the frame revealing a front-page press photo of Meghan in her Kinguyakkii outfit of a ski cap, oversized parka, pointing at something off camera and looking determined. The headline read: Chief Nabs Murderer.

The rest of the article could wait. Meghan received the framed item and immediately turned it to face the back of the stage.

"Chief Sheppard," Calvin said with a proud grin. "Thank you for showing us you're willing to do whatever it takes to make sure justice is served."

"Speaking of serving justice," Dead-Air Dave broke in, leaning over the microphone. "We can't serve anything without the right ingredients."

"Chief Sheppard," White-Noise Wayne chimed in, "From all of us at KING-AM Radio—"

"Best radio station on top of the world!" Dave injected for a fresh round of cheers.

"We'd like to present you with our gift," Wayne continued. He produced a large plastic tub of creamy peanut butter. It was an industrial-sized container with a handle, ribbon, and bow. When he started to hand it to Meghan while the crowd cheered, Wayne pulled back before she could take the twenty-five pound container. He leaned to the microphone and asked, "You don't have an allergy, do you?"

It was more than she ever expected. Meghan was involved in the apprehension of bad guys before. She'd never received any special treatment for doing a job that came easy for her. It was a strange sensation that took her as much a surprise as the recognition she received that night.

"You have anything to say?" Dave asked.

Meghan glanced to Duane. He was smiling in a way that politicians did when they were in front of a crowd. He clapped with the audience, but somehow his hands weren't making much noise.

Meghan handed the tub of peanut butter to Duane, so he'd stop pretending. Rolling the loose strands of coppery hair behind her ear, Meghan cleared her throat and leaned toward the open microphone.

"Whoever is stealing aviation fuel from the airport, you better stop now, or I am going to arrest you."

Everyone went quiet, absorbing the warning. Only Oliver clapped and cheered. She saw him stand beside Vincent Atkinson, looking sheepish.

"Well, let's hope whoever it is doesn't have a peanut allergy," Dave added to keep the crowd amped up. The delivery came with another round of applause. Meghan took her exit. Calvin was there at the base of the stage, helping her down again.

She left the framed article leaning against a stack of chairs, facing away from the crowd. It was a proud moment, a great piece, but a terrible picture of Meghan. The tub of peanut butter sat beside the portrait.

"So, what'd you think?" he asked.

"I feel like this got away from everyone on why we're all here," she admitted.

"Not at all," Calvin said. "Look around a see a roomful of happy people. Even the Snyders are having a good time. Death is a part of life. We have a different view of death in Alaska. It's been so long since I've been to a wake or funeral in the lower-forty-eight that I can't compare the two, but here we like thinking about life because it can end at any moment."

"I like that." She scanned the crowd. "Congratulations on the *Associated Press*."

"I couldn't have done it without you."

"So, it made national news."

"I got a call from a couple of Anchorage news stations. I even got a call from a cable news network. They're calling me to get to you."

"I'm not interested."

"It's good for the town, you know. If you did an interview," he said in a subtle plead.

"I just want to do my job without all the attention."

"Does this have anything to do with what happened to you before?"

For a guy who wanted to keep the festivities cheerful, Calvin managed to pick the one point that was still raw for Meghan, even after all the years. "I'll tell you about it sometime. Right now, let's enjoy the evening."

There was more music; some took the opportunity to dance. The DJs competed with each other trying to get Meghan to dance with them. She explained while she was out of uniform, she wasn't off-duty. It seemed to work. She was content to hang back, shake hands when people wandered close to her, and have pleasant conversations that had nothing to do with peanut butter.

Chapter Thirty-Four

That night when Meghan went home, she removed the smartphone from her clutch purse. She'd turned down the ringer because she wanted a few hours of being a woman instead of a cop. Sometimes even the little things mattered. She liked the attention; some who gave her focus was more welcome than others.

The framed front page of the newspaper leaned against the wall in front of the collection of cardboard boxes. She'd left it facing out and wasn't sure what she was going to do with it. The pastor from the local nondenominational church gratefully accepted the donation of the giant tub of peanut butter. There was one church in town. The pastor was a progressive man who thought it was better to bring people together instead of worrying about whose god was bigger and better. It worked for the villagers. He organized the local food pantry and Wednesday night soup feed for subsistent families who didn't have a lot. Everyone in town seemed to find a way to work together as an extended family instead of neighbors who didn't care about each other.

The article made national news. There were missed calls from numbers she didn't recognize when she scanned the call logs. The voicemail was full. News personalities wanted interviews. The *Associated Press* published the article on Friday, the day before Nancy's celebration of life at the civic center. She got a good look at the photograph. It wasn't half-bad. She looked a little tired. Meghan felt she looked rugged, a representation to the rest of the women to not be afraid to dress warmly when she was in cold weather. It was the woman's prerogative to sacrifice warmth for fashion.

Meghan saw her ex-husband called but hadn't left a voicemail. Brittany called four times and left a volume of texts for Meghan to get in touch with her immediately. The word got out. Her daughter knew the last time she'd talked to her mother she had a run-in with a murderer who almost took Meghan's life. A lot of the article glossed over the events around her physical ordeal with Hodge, and for that, she was grateful to Calvin for exercising journalistic restraint.

Stepping out of the dress, slipping it back on the hanger and throwing a plastic garment bag over it for another occasion, Meghan put the dress back into the closet. Maybe she'd get an opportunity to wear it again.

Since she already wore leggings, she found a sweatshirt, slipped it on, and in a half second, unlatched her bra and pulled it off. Now she could breathe, was comfortable, and when the time came, Meghan could slip into bed.

When the phone buzzed, she saw another text from her daughter. Looking at the clock, seeing it was after eight in Alaska, it was after midnight in New York. The text was brief, asked her to call as soon as she could.

Since Meghan was still awake, she crawled into bed and dialed the number.

"Is your phone broken?" were the first words from her daughter.

"No, I've been a little busy. I see you're still awake. Are you spending the night at a friend's house?" Meghan put her head against the pillow and lay in the dark. The contact photo of Brittany glowed; the smartphone rested against the pillow beside Meghan. She could lay there, facing her daughter and talk to her like they used to do when Brittany was a little girl and full of questions that only Mommy could answer.

"I think you've been more than a little busy," Brittany scolded.

"What do you mean?" Meghan suspected what she meant.

"I heard about what happened. I saw something on the news about it. You caught some deranged killer in the Alaskan wild."

"That sounds a little over the top to me."

"Are you kidding me? The last time I talked to you, you said you were busy, and that's why you couldn't talk to me on that Saturday. You were catching a killer."

"Well, it wasn't like that." She tucked her hands under her face, watching the phone. They had the technology to talk face to face on video conference through the phone. Sometimes it worked; sometimes it lagged and ended the call. At least with the cell phone speaker on, she could still hear Brittany, and the picture was still as beautiful as she remembered. "I was busy investigating the crime scene that Saturday."

"What happened, was it all gross, did he like, use a knife?"

"Where are you?"

"I'm home."

"Okay." She sighed. "I'm not giving you details that don't matter."

"Is it because you're investigating another murder?"

"No, I'm home, lying in bed actually, talking to you." Meghan thought about the case file she brought home. Detective Anderson wanted her to look at it. She hadn't dug into it yet because Meghan wished to enjoy the quiet for a minute or two.

"Remember when you put me to bed, and it felt like I stayed up late asking you all sorts of questions?"

Meghan smiled. "Yes, I remember that. I'm surprised you remember."

"I remember."

"You didn't stay up very long. Mostly you fell asleep about ten minutes after you went to bed."

"It felt like forever." She paused. Meghan suspected Brittany had something to talk to her about but hadn't found the path to lead into a conversation. "I was thinking about trying out for track next year?"

"Really? That's awesome."

"Yeah, I like running, I think if I had an excuse to run, I'd do it more."

"You've got long legs, and you're taller than me. You get that from your Dad's side of the family."

"Well, the coach wants us to start training this summer."

"Oh," Meghan heard it. There it was, the lead into a conversation that her daughter wanted to have but didn't know how to broach. "Well, it makes sense. You start running during the summer, you can build up your endurance before school starts, and you train to compete."

"Yeah, I guess so."

"Listen, I understand, Brittany. You want to stay there this summer and start your training."

202

"Well, actually, I was wondering if there's anywhere to run up there."

"Here? In town?"

"Yeah, that crazy town you live in, King—Gi—I—Ki—I," Brittany pronounced slowly.

"It's Kinguyakkii," Meghan said.

"Kinguyakkii," Brittany repeated.

"That's good, sounds natural." She took a deep breath to slow her heart from thumping out of her chest. "So, you want to come up here this summer?"

"Well, yeah. Maybe I can start training up there. Is the air thinner there? Like I could get high-altitude training."

"We're pretty close to sea-level. Kinguyakkii is right on the shore of the bay."

"Oh, okay." Brittany sounded unsure. It was healthy, people thought of Alaska in terms of 'up there,' and that geographic idea came with height. "So, do you think if I came up there, I could run?"

"Of course, you could. I'll make a deal with you. I'll run with you. It will give me an excuse to get back into shape."

"Yeah, you probably need it."

"Listen, just because you're my daughter doesn't mean you can be brutally honest with me."

"I saw your picture online. I read the article the local reporter wrote. I saw his picture too in the byline. He's cute. Is he single?"

"What about my picture?"

"You look like a total badass in that shot."

203

"Well, it must have been the lighting."

Brittany paused again. It seemed like the minutes ticked away. "Did you almost die?"

Meghan swallowed. She'd read the article. Calvin was kind with the details surrounding the arrest...well, Hodge's takedown. He wrote about the altercation. It wasn't a secret that she fought with the killer.

"I'm here. It happened."

"Aren't you scared? I mean, I'd be scared."

"You're tough, and you'd be surprised what you can do when you put your mind to it. You don't give yourself enough credit. You ready to come up here then?"

"Yeah, I am. Is it pretty?"

"It's gorgeous. People see picturesque parts of Alaska. When you come to a place like Kinguyakkii, there's no sugar-coating. This is real Alaska. The weather can change in an hour, and ice fog can sock-in the town. But you keep going and eventually, everything works out again. I think you'll like it."

"Yeah, some of my friends say they want to go."

"I've never met anyone who hasn't said they'd like to visit Alaska. When you come, you can give them the real dirt on it."

"Are you really okay? I'm worried something's going to happen to you."

"I'm okay, Sweetie. It doesn't happen here. It's not like before."

"I don't want to talk about that."

"I know, I'm sorry," Meghan said. Brittany's perception of the events that got her mother shot was from the outside looking in on the incident. "I'm still here. I know it feels like you're a million miles away, but I'm still here. You can call anytime you want; you know that.

"I never know what time it is there. That's why I texted you. Dad wants me to visit you."

"Does he? That's cool." She refused to engage in any negative conversations with her daughter about her ex-husband. That was something Meghan had never exposed her daughter to, and she felt better for it. "Well, I'll send him an email with a tentative schedule for the summer. We get everything worked out; we'll get you the plane ticket. You'll have to fly solo."

"Yeah, I know. It doesn't sound so bad."

"I like flying solo; makes you feel cool."

"You're a dork, Mom."

"I know, but I'm your dork."

"I love you. I'm a little scared for you now after reading that article."

"It's worse than it was," Meghan said and felt as if she'd lied to her daughter. "Honestly, there hasn't been a murder here in fifteen years."

"Did they get who did it? Is there some crazy madman running around in the wilderness?"

"There are a few interesting people out there. They didn't get who did it, but I'm pretty sure here is a lot safer than there."

"I feel safe here."

"That's good, and there's no reason why you shouldn't." Meghan pressed the back of her wrist against her mouth, trying to suppress the yawn that suddenly showed up.

"Is it late there?" Brittany asked.

"No, not really, remember I'm four hours behind you."

"Oh, okay. I'm tired too."

"Well, I'll let you go. Get some sleep."

"I miss you," Brittany said, she sniffled.

"Oh, Honey, I miss you too."

"You like it there?" She attempted to ask Meghan to leave Alaska and come back to her.

"I love it here. You know, I wasn't running away from you when I moved here. You know that, right? I needed a change after everything that happened. I wanted something different, and I wanted to go somewhere I felt like I mattered like I made a difference. It feels like I make a difference here."

"I'm not going to guilt you into leaving there, Mom. I think it's cool. I just miss you."

"I'm here. And I'll see you in a couple of months."

"I know." It was Brittany's turn to yawn.

"All right, time for bed. I love you."

"Goodnight, Mom."

"Night, Brittany."

They ended the call. Meghan lay facing the dark face of the smartphone for a little while. She pressed her fingers against her eyes to push back the tears. In a few months, Brittany would be here. They'd go running together, she'd fall in love with the place the way Meghan had, and it would feel as if everything was right in the world. She just had to wait, do her job, and know that this kind of thing, a murder in a rural village in bush Alaska doesn't happen every day. *It's not like a series or anything*, Meghan thought, then put the phone on the nightstand and rolled over to go to sleep.

Made in the USA
Monee, IL
31 May 2020

32260671R00115